Lola,
Death Awaits You at the End of the Street

and Other Stories

LOLA DEATH Awaits You at the End of the of the Street

and Other Stories

Lola,
Death Awaits You at the End of the Street
and Other Stories

Pnina Tel Dan

Traklin Pninim, Publishing, Maale Adumim 2024

Pnina Tel Dan

**Lola, Death Awaits You at the End of the Street
and Other Stories**

First Edition

Translated from Hebrew by Yaron Regev

Cover design by Iser L. Hershkowitz
Editing by Stanley D. Hartzvi

Typesetting, layout and production - Traklin Pninim, Publishing

Traklin Pninim, Maale Adumim, 2024

To the man of my life, to the man by my side,
To Reuben, my husband for almost half a century,
Beloved, friend and partner on the journey of life,
For better and for worse,
For eternity,
Thank you

Love
[1]Two fish hurried and
descended to the depths of the sea
to tell each other
how great their love was.

────────────────────

[1]Ravikovitch, Dahlia. "Love of a Golden Apple": 'Love', Sifriat Poalim, Published by HaKibbutz HaArtzi HaShomer HaTzair, 1976, p. 51

Contents

Pnina Tel Dan

His Desire is Toward Her

Yom Kippur. Outside, the sounds of running feet and neighbors' cries fill the air. The door swings wide open, and for a moment, Munch's *The Scream* seems to echo through it. Yossi rushes inside and turns on the radio transistor: "This is The Voice of Israel broadcasting from Jerusalem. It is now three o'clock, *gmar chatima tova*." Aryeh Golan's urgent voice invades the room: "The IDF — The Israel Defense Forces, spokesperson reports that just before two this afternoon, Egyptian and Syrian forces launched a widespread attack in the Sinai Peninsula and the Golan Heights. Our forces are actively engaging the attackers."

My brother dons his uniform, hurriedly stuffing whatever he can grab into his tattered duffle bag, then says his goodbyes to me and our elderly parents: "War has broken out; I need to return to base. I must hitch rides to Sinai. Take care of yourselves."

"What will become of Yossi? When will we see him again? May God keep him safe from harm," my mother murmurs. My father, thunderstruck, sways where he stands. In a desperate attempt to steady himself, he grabs the white tablecloth. The festive tableware set for our end-of-fast meal slowly slides and crashes to the floor, shattering our hopes for a '*gmar chatima tova*' — that we be sealed in the book of life.

Even as he leaves, another arrives. At six o'clock, as we watch Golda Meir speak, a knock sounds at the door. Dafna (our Daffi), clad in her Gadna uniform, enters. Dafna finished her studies a year and a half ago and has been guiding the Gadna youth pre-military program for my class ever since. She completed her national service at Soroka Hospital and has been studying nursing at Ben-Gurion University for six months. Her practical studies are conducted at Soroka Hospital, where I volunteer.

"Good evening, sorry for the interruption. Vicky, your class is volunteering at Soroka Hospital. Hurry, the car is waiting outside."

My father "gets up on his hind legs", his voice muffled but firm, "I'm sorry, Dafna, but Vicky is only fifteen. She isn't going anywhere. She's staying right here with her parents."

Dafna shakes her head, her fiery hair lashing out and brushing against the officer ranks on her shoulders. "I'm sorry, Vicky's father, but the high school principal has determined that all Gadna classes are to assist in the war effort. Vicky, who volunteers with the MDA, has been assigned to Soroka Hospital."

Before my father can embarrass me further, I quickly interject, "I'll be coming in a second."

I hastily pack a few clothes and toiletries into my jean bag and slip away from my father's bear hug. I make sure not to look back, lest my mother's sorrow and tears turn me into a pillar of salt.

"Hey, girl, running away from home?"

I know Yaron is joking. I bow my head, and my black curls fall forward, shielding the flush creeping up my neck and spreading across my face. I remain silent.

Everyone knows Yaron Partosh, the commanding officer of the Gadna at our high school, who graduated with honors a year ago and volunteered for a year of community service in Beersheba's struggling neighborhood D. He's aware of my volunteer work with MDA — Magen David Adom, Israel's National Emergency Pre-Hospital Medical and Blood Services Organization, which has prepared me somewhat for what lies ahead at Soroka Hospital.

We arrive at the hospital at sundown. Tents have been set up on the wide lawn to accommodate the myriad of young volunteers. Radio transistors blare news updates alongside recruitment slogans for reserve units, and songs play continuously: "I'll Wait for You," "No Need to Worry," "Let It Be."

We rush into a large hall transformed into a makeshift triage center to receive the injured expected from Sinai via the helipad.

The injured start flooding in from the very first night. Their agonizing cries, the burnt smell, the blood, and the grim scenes quickly dispel any youthful joy. We work in silence, bent and somber, helping to evacuate the wounded and assist the medical staff.

On the third day, the flow of casualties markedly increases, and around midnight, we encounter a young soldier severely wounded in the frontal lobe. His dirty bandage slips from his forehead, revealing wounds visible beneath his blood-soaked black locks. Despite the transfusions and painkillers, he writhes in agony. Lying on his side, his lower back is torn and peppered with shrapnel. He doesn't know his name; no identification tags are found. Daffi looks at him, and his blue eyes meet hers with fear and pain. He reaches out his hand to hers, and she responds gently, holding his hand to comfort him.

I lose all sense of time, each day blurring into the next. I assist the nurses in the neurological ward, changing bed linens, distributing food and letters. In the evenings, I join the others at the helipad to help transfer the wounded to the emergency room.

***

Yesterday, after helping Yaron transfer a man with injured limbs to the orthopedic ward, I felt the earth slipping from under my feet. It was eleven o'clock at night. For two whole weeks, I had been unable to sleep due to the horrific sights of charred injured bodies squeezing into my bed. A buzzing in my ears began, I wobbled and then fell. Yaron softened my fall and cradled me in his muscular arms.

"Tell me, when was the last time you ate a decent meal? Are you getting any sleep at all? I see you running around all the time."

"I don't remember," I whispered, still unsteady.

Without many words, Yaron led me to the cafeteria and bought us both shakshuka. We wolfed it down with challah bread and washed it down with a large cup of cocoa.

"Look, I don't care about the war right now. We are going to get some sleep, recharge, and reset."

In the corridor near the cardiology ward, we found an empty bed. We lay down, and I tried to sleep. The moment I closed my eyes, amputated, charred bodies tried to squeeze in with us on the narrow bed. Yaron saw my discomfort, wrapped his arms around me, and commanded, "Sleep." A comforting scent of pine needles filled my nostrils.

Overcome by exhaustion, without any self-control or awareness, I pressed as close to him as possible and buried my face in the hollow of his neck.

"You smell so good," I said indulgently.

"Stop with the nonsense," he ordered again. "I'll sing you a song, and you'll fall asleep from boredom in no time: 'Cloudless skies, a yawning moon, a hot cup of coffee, a toast with melted cheese, the wisps of smoke from a thin cigarette. A pleasant tiredness descends upon you. A beautiful girl falls into her sleep.'"

He repeated these silly lines like a whispered mantra, holding me tightly, and his pleasant scent became my refuge. The charred bodies slept with us, all fitting in one bed.

The next morning, I woke up smiling, hungry, and lovesick in an empty bed. I searched for Yaron amid the hectic assignments but couldn't find him. It had been his last day with us. Due to the war, he was drafted earlier, and I never saw him again.

At noon, as I returned the clean bedding to the neurological ward, I saw Daffi washing the blue-eyed soldier, trying to lighten his mood and distract him from his pain.

After two weeks of surgeries removing shrapnel from his head and back, he still couldn't remember who he was or his own name.

For him, only the present existed. Daffi was his entire world, his anchor. She cared for him devotedly, bathing him, changing his dressings, feeding him, and taking him for walks on the hospital lawns in his wheelchair. She made sure to talk to him and importantly, refrained from pestering him with intrusive questions about his elusive past. She called him "pretty-eyed David," and he called her "my beloved Abishag."

I often saw them growing close, cuddling. Initially, Daffi resisted his advances, but she soon let down her guard and surrendered completely to their love.

In the third week of the war, during one of my rounds delivering mail, I heard shouting and heartrending cries from the corridor outside David's room.

"What do you want from me? Leave me alone."

"Raffi, it's me, Tamara, your wife. We've been married for two years. And this is Gil, our son. He's six months old. We love you, and we've been so worried about you. Everyone is waiting for you to come back — your family, your students, our friends at the kibbutz."

"I don't know you, and I certainly wouldn't have married someone like you. You're not my type. Do me a favor, don't try to pin a baby on me. I have a girlfriend. Her name is Daffi, understand? This is Daffi, my girlfriend. Daffi, meet this strange woman who I can't understand what she wants from me."

"David, I mean Raffi, stop shouting at her. You're scaring the baby, your son Gili. Please, stop!" Daffi pleaded, her voice choked with tears. She was deeply unnerved by these shocking revelations, overwhelmed.

"Daffi, please stay out of this. Let me handle this nuisance alone."

"Raffi, please," the woman also pleaded, "try to remember. It's only a matter of time and patience. And I have the patience, I'll wait."

"I don't want to see you. Get out of my sight," he roared.

Tamar's crying intensified. She left the room, leaning against the corridor wall. The sweet baby she clasped in her arms wept as well. Her legs buckled, and she collapsed onto the corridor floor.

Whispers emanated from inside the room. Osnat, the social worker, emerged into the corridor. She bent down to Tamar and helped her to her feet. Offering hugs and comfort, she escorted Tamar out until they both vanished from my view.

Near the room, on the floor, I spotted a crumpled piece of paper. I picked it up. It was torn and obviously part of an official document. Driven by curiosity, I read what was written on it:

"In the first week of the war, a soldier was brought to the hospital with injuries to his lower back and head trauma. An inquiry by the casualty officer revealed that he belonged to one of the tank companies that fought at the Suez Canal. The soldier was identified as the company's second-in-command, Lieutenant Raffi Tzabar. He was the sole survivor of a brutal battle in which his entire tank company was destroyed.

Raffi's physical condition has improved, but due to the head injuries, he suffers from amnesia. He cannot remember anything about his past or his identity, and he experiences violent outbursts typical of post-traumatic stress disorder.

Raffi is being treated […]."

I glanced into the room whose door remained open and saw David, Raffi, pulling Dafna towards him. She couldn't stop crying. He tried to embrace her in the shelter of their bed, in a desperate attempt to comfort her and recreate their shattered bubble of happiness.

Was it real life or just fantasy

"Sustain me with Raisins and Wine;
Refresh me with Apples,
For I am sick with love."

Ruby

Leonard Cohen's voice, more cracked than life itself, oozed from Roni and Rinat's living room, stroking against Ruby:

"Dance me to your beauty
with a burning violin."

The love-brimming sounds stirred a longing within him for something missing, perhaps a promise to fulfill an unnamed, elusive desire:

"Dance me through the panic
till I'm gathered safely in."

Ruby leaned on the balcony rail overlooking the sea. The wind caught each tender sound, flung them into the waves, and returned them, revived and haunting, to wet his clothes, teasing him with the illusion of a secret promise.

"Rinat, do me a favor. This nightmare with Amnon is still fresh. I don't need anything. Did you invite me here just for this? What's wrong? If you're suffering, does everyone have to suffer with you? I don't understand why everyone who falls into the marriage trap feels obligated to drag their friends down too. Go find someone else to make miserable."

"Paula, shut up. You're unbearable. If Ruby hears you, he'll be offended and pull away. Look, it's just like riding a bike. You fall, you get back up, and you keep going."

"Listen, Rinat, I never learned to ride a bike. So your clichés are wasted on me. I'm going back to my aunt's house. I've had enough. All these dim red lights, the incense, Leonard Cohen's sultry voice, the sound of the waves... How much more pathetic can you get? Have you opened a brothel? Ever since you got married, your boredom and idleness have led you to meddle in my life? Pimp me out? Enough already, Rinat. Move on to Dinah. She'd swoon in Ruby's arms, melt like butter."

Ruby, overhearing the loud conversation, turned just in time to catch Paula's final sentences.

What drew him to her, even before seeing her face, was not her words but how she spoke them, especially the tone and timbre of her voice. There was something hauntingly familiar about it, reminiscent of Ilesh from the novel *Grotesque*. Without hesitation, he approached them.

"Hello, I'm Ruby. Since Rinat has gone to such lengths to create this whole romantic atmosphere, we might as well make the most of it. Dinah isn't really my type. So, perhaps we could try instead. Shall we dance?"

Before Paula could react, she found herself in his embrace. Lenny's words, "Hold me tight," pressed her close to him. They danced silently, their bodies relaxed and intertwined, as if they had always been close, swaying to the alluring tones of Lenny's voice.

At the end of the dance, still dazed by their immediate connection and enveloped in silence, they stepped out onto the balcony, the twilight atmosphere making it hard to see each other. There, they sat like old friends, enjoying the sea breeze, the music, and above all, the comforting silence, the sense of home that wrapped around them.

Ruby lost all sense of reality, and honestly, his bearings too. It was hard for him to gauge how long they had been wrapped in their silent cocoon. Had they been absent forever, or was it just half an hour? He felt the ground slip from beneath his feet, overcome by a mix of confusion and dizziness. The tranquility dissipated, replaced by something both unsettling and enticing. He decided it was best to leave on a high note, even though he hadn't clearly seen her face or had a meaningful conversation with her.

"Tomorrow, I'm returning to the base. I have a meeting at nine at Hatzerim. I'm sorry. I'll get your address from your aunt. I'll find you, I promise."

Before she could object, he bent down, kissed her cheek, and left.

Paula

"So, I couldn't care less about that Ruby..." Rinat imitated Paula half-mockingly. "As if. I thought I'd need a spatula to scrape you off him. You two looked like 'El and Elat,' those mythical beings woven together into a dual-headed god of love. Bound never to part, in life or in death. But tell me, dumbass, how did you let him escape like that?" she teased.

"Cut it out. I'll probably never see him again. And if I do, would I even recognize him? In that pitch darkness, I could've easily gotten pregnant and not recognized the father the next day. For heaven's sake, Rinat, turn on some lights. I swear, I don't even know what your Ruby looks like. Who he even is. He said he'd get my address from my aunt... Dumbest thing I've ever heard. I bet I'll never see him again. And you, Rinat, do yourself a favor and keep your day job because matchmaking and playing Madame aren't your strengths. We didn't even make out."

"Didn't make out, huh? I've never danced so closely with anyone, not even with Roni, and we've been married for six months. What exactly did you two do on the balcony in the dark for an hour? Count stars?"

"We kept quiet. It was fun. So much fun that I was caught off guard, and he slipped away. What's this nonsense about him taking my address from Aunt Sarah? Where did that even come from…"

"He's the neighbor from the villa across the street, opposite your aunt's. She's been the dentist for his whole family for years. Ruby is a friend of Roni from the army. So, don't worry, my dear, mommy will take care of you. Did you guys make any plans in Beersheba?"

"Didn't I just tell you the guy ran off? How could we have made plans? Whether he knows my aunt or not, I bet this was the last time I'll ever see him."

"Nonsense, Paula. You wouldn't recognize a good thing even if it was right in front of you, close enough to touch. Ruby is a senior officer at the Hatzerim Airbase, a graduate of the Air Force Technical School. He's a brilliant guy, interested in robotics and science fiction. A bookworm just like you and loves movies. He plans to study physics. He noticed you last year when we were at the Sahne Park. He had a girlfriend then, Lydia. Did you know her? He even asked about you back then, while your head was buried in '*Love in the Time of Cholera.*' No wonder you didn't notice him. But he definitely saw you.

Though I'm not sure he got a good look at your face. You know, in that red bikini of yours, it's hard for anyone to focus on anything else. So, I'm not sure he'd recognize you when you open the door."

"Very funny. But if by some miracle he does knock on my door, I won't be the one opening it. I'm staying in Caesarea for another two weeks. I don't feel like sweating to death in the mid-August sauna that Beersheba turns into. If he's smart, he'll come back to spend the weekend near the Caesarea aqueduct. There, among the waves, he might find his Aphrodite enjoying the breeze. That's it, I'm off to my aunt's. So bye, Rinat, see you tomorrow at the beach."

Sweet is the Apple

Twilight draped the lush Hadar Carmel neighborhood park, bordered by trees. At its foothills, far below, the lights of the beach twinkled like precious gems. The sun struggled in its final throes of dimming light before succumbing to its Sisyphean death in the sea's darkness. Above, through the velvety, starry heavens, Lucy sparkled in the sky with a wink of diamonds. Ruby embraced Paula, and she rested her head on his shoulder. He alternately bit into a green apple and kissed her fruity lips. The apple's bittersweet nectar was shared between them. Paula recalled a line from a Dahlia Ravikovitch poem: *"An orange, consumed by the man who ate it, invaded his skin to the flesh beneath."*[2]

---

[2] Ravikovitch, Dahlia. "Love of a Golden Apple": 'Love of a Golden Apple', Sifriat Poalim, Published by HaKibbutz HaArtzi HaShomer HaTzair, 1976, p. 5

Ruby stood from the bench and pulled Paula to him. Together, they spread a dark blue wool blanket on a grass clearing that had formed as if from nowhere among the trees of a Mediterranean grove, in their own private Wuthering Heights.

The morning after the party, Ruby approached Micha Sagiv, the flight academy's deputy commander. Two weeks earlier, Sagiv had scheduled a work meeting to discuss the aeronautics course curriculum that he had asked Ruby to teach to the base cadets immediately after the holidays. Now, Ruby used the opportunity to redeem all the vacation days he had accumulated since becoming a standing officer at the base.

The vacation was set to end on Sunday, and they spent all eight days on nature hikes in the Hadar Carmel area, lounging on the beach in Haifa, and frolicking among the waves in Caesarea.

During their hikes, they walked softly, step by step, even in vulnerable areas, within each other's protected nature reserves. They sought to deepen their intimacy, breaking through fortified walls and defenses they had built around themselves.

Each exploration ended with strenuous journeys to uncover the mysteries of their bodies. Like seasoned scouts, they traced every sign in the quest to maximize pleasure.

Tomorrow, Ruby would return to the base and wouldn't see Paula for another two weeks. The imminent separation stirred a potent mix of sexual tension and primal passion, rooted in fear of abandonment. They pondered whether the intimacy they had developed was genuine or just a fleeting summer romance.

They lay on the blanket in the middle of the clearing. The dark velvet sky almost touched their exposed skin. Lucy sent her love from above once again.

Paula placed her hand on Ruby's chest and traced his skin's textures with her fingertips, attempting to draw out all the words that could capture what she felt. With their eyes closed, she paused upon reaching his abdomen, encountering an obstacle. They both gasped, their breaths mingling with the sounds of the grove and the rustling wind.

Her hand grasped his masculinity, and his arms enveloped her body. They entwined, blurring where she ended and he began. His lips thirsted for hers; their breaths intertwined. His tender kisses fluttered up her neck, revealing all her vulnerabilities, causing uncontrollable tremors — a desire to escape her skin, abandon her body, scream from pain and pleasure alike. Leaping into the void, into a complete loss of senses, they sought release from the vortex of unbearable pleasure.

His hands continued their topographical discoveries, exploring her body's contours — fingertips gliding over peaks and through valleys, at times touching, then hovering, caressing, and stroking.

Their bodies wove into one, their movements as rhythmic and harmonious as the waves crescendoing against the shore — crashing, retreating, then surging back with even greater force. His tongue acted as a rearguard, ensuring all landmarks were acknowledged. He wanted to make sure they would reach the coveted destination at just the right place and time for both of them.

***

Two weeks had passed, and still, Paula had not heard from Ruby. He hadn't called or written. Memories of Caesarea, the aqueduct, Hadar Carmel, and Lucy, along with their intimate explorations, were beginning to fade from her mind.

The end-of-summer aridity of the Negev's dusty capital gnawed at her spirit. *I must have made much ado about nothing,* she thought. She had felt like Amerigo Vespucci, but America, whose shores she had thrilled to discover, had long been explored by Ruby with others.

She rose and placed a Leonard Cohen record on the turntable. She had purchased it at the end of last summer with the money she earned from picking oranges at Kibbutz Dvir, along with a collection of other records.

This was her third consecutive summer spent picking oranges. While her friends traveled to the beach, Eilat, or abroad, living life to the fullest, she had persisted, worked tirelessly. Now, she sought solace in her Lenny's lyrics, asking her to hold him tight. In Ruby's complete absence, this was her meager comfort, though some might call it a fool's solace. Earlier, she had listened to The Beatles, who seemed to send warm greetings from Lucy, now more distant and unreachable than ever.

The shrill ringing of the doorbell abruptly interrupted her thoughts. Paula waited, expecting one of her housemates to answer, but then remembered she was alone. She silenced the music, quickly pulled on some shorts and a black tank top, and went to see who was disrupting her blues.

At the door stood Ruby, leaning on the doorframe, covered in dust, his lips cracked, a goofy smile plastered across his face. "You live right in the middle of nowhere," he said. "I've been looking for 3 Alfred Rosi Street since this morning. It's noon now. I found you purely by chance. No one seems to know this street. You don't understand, Paula, I haven't had anything to drink. I'm dying of thirst."

Ruby attempted to restore some dignity to his dusty summer Air Force uniform. He brushed off the dust, tucked his shirt into his trousers, and tightened his belt.

Paula pulled him inside, and between kisses and hugs, she ushered him to her disheveled bed and rushed to the kitchen to fetch him some water before he wilted from dehydration right in front of her.

She returned with a pitcher of cold water with floating lemon slices and a large packet of petit beurre biscuits. She clumsily dumped the biscuits onto a too-small plate; most fell onto the square wooden table, and a few rolled onto the floor.

After he drank some water and sprawled out on her bed, Ruby flicked a few biscuit crumbs into the opening of her tank top and joked about her poor hospitality.

Imitating the Egyptian movies so popular at the time, he burst into mock pathos-filled dialogue:

"I'm starving, and she brings me biscuits. How will you feed our children, eh, my Jasmine, my love?" he concluded with a chuckle, purring like a cat pleased with his own cleverness.

With a smile of her own, Paula quickly slipped into her role: "Ahmed, *ya ayuni*, heart of my heart, I brought our children into the world; the least you could do is feed them!" And she splashed a little ice water from the pitcher onto his smiling face.

"Alright, my Farhana, my love, come, *ya binti,* your Ahmed will make us a small Arabic salad, a vegetable omelet, and coffee with milk, so he will have enough prowess in his loins to fill our tent with little Jasmines and Ahmeds."

After enjoying a delicious brunch and returning to her room, Paula handed Ruby a clean towel and urged him to take a shower

— to wash off the dust and sweat clinging to him — so that they could finally enjoy the dessert they had both eagerly anticipated for the past two weeks.

I am Sick with Love, and Ruby?

Paula lay on the grass at the university, in front of the Faculty of Natural Sciences. The spring sun caressed her bare legs. She rested her head on her denim backpack, filled with her books and the day's lecture notes. She watched the ever-changing shapes of the grayish-white clouds above, trying to decipher what they masqueraded as. It was one past noon, and she had two free hours. Her belly, not yet showing her second pregnancy, sent her signals of discomfort. She was hungry. Don wouldn't need picking up from kindergarten until five. She had a couple of hours until her last lecture of the day. So, she decided to bask in the day's warmth and let the comforting sun penetrate her skin, soothe her. She resolved to yield to the gentle breeze's flirting, to be caressed by it and to feel content.

And yet, despite her resolution, a nagging discomfort began to intrude on her peace and happiness. Something was still not right — an unclear inner feeling of discontent.

Was she truly happy? Doubts about her life with Ruby and their love began to surface. As usual, these doubts led her to perform her ritual inventory check, which always alleviated her worries: *I am twenty-three, married to Ruby for three years, a handsome, intelligent man studying for his master's degree in physics. My husband excels in his studies and has recently secured a position as a teaching assistant. I am the mother of our adorable two-year-old Don. I am soon to graduate cum laude with degrees in literature and philosophy, along with a teaching certificate. I am pregnant again, and this time, it's the daughter I wished for. Last month, Ruby and I bought a four-room apartment on Masada Road. I write short stories and plan to delve into literary research. We are healthy, thank God, and we love each other passionately, as much as when we first met.*

In the first two years of their marriage, they could hardly keep their hands off each other. They stayed awake, holding each other after every lovemaking session, talking into the early hours as they did on the day they first met, needing to say everything before parting. Paula couldn't understand what caused this pervasive feeling of something lacking, accompanied by a gnawing sadness and a type of fear, and why even her ritual 'inventory check', which usually had a calming effect, failed to dispel it.

Sometimes, when she opened her eyes — always about half an hour after Ruby had awakened and made her comforting Saturday morning coffee — a poem he had written for her awaited on his pillow. She didn't know when or why the poems had stopped. This year, even their good morning kiss seemed to have vanished. Often, she recalled that sense of something missing in her life only in the middle of the day.

When she shared this with Dahlia, her confidante, the latter smiled dismissively, waved her hand, and mockingly said, "Are you serious, Paula? You expect to remain a lovesick girl forever, even after three years of marriage? Okay, I get it, you're madly in love with Ruby, and he probably loves you no less. But come on, Paula, you have a two-year-old son. Wake up. Do you think life is just about birds chirping, butterfly wings fluttering, and the scent of roses? Hasn't the stench of Don's diapers opened your eyes yet?"

Paula vividly remembered that conversation. It was essentially the last serious conversation she had had with Dahlia.

She was upset by her friend's lack of empathy and her dismissive attitude towards her struggles. But that wasn't the only thing that had altered their once symbiotic relationship.

A dark cloud had passed between them since that Saturday morning "misunderstanding" at Paula's parents' house. She and Ruby had come to visit her parents and stayed the entire weekend. On Saturday, Dahlia visited, and they caught up, talking about books they had read and friends who had enlisted, listening to their favorite records as if nothing had changed. They planned to go out together for a hike out in nature. Paula excused herself to get ready while asking Ruby to entertain Dahlia.

When she opened the door of her room to rejoin Ruby and Dahlia, unusually, the voice of Arik Einstein singing *"San Francisco on the Water"* stung her ears, as if burning her skin.

She entered the room with Don clutching the hem of her shirt. At first, she couldn't comprehend what she was seeing: Dahlia leaning on the desk with Ruby close behind her, almost embracing her as they read together from a book lying open on the desk, *"Grotesque."*

The creak of the door being opened startled the two people dearest to her. They abruptly parted from each other. Paula remained in the doorway, her eyes brimming with tears, clouded by a mix of indignation and anger. "It seems you two went on your own excursion without us. I'm sure you must be tired. I think I'll skip the hike and go to sleep. Maybe after I wake up, I'll be convinced this was all just a bad dream," she said in a choked voice.

Without giving them another look, before they could respond, she retreated to her parents' bedroom, clutching Don in her arms. Dahlia left without saying goodbye, and since then, Paula had neither seen her nor heard from her.

Paula tried to reach out, especially after Ruby denied her interpretation of what she had seen, explaining that her eyes had deceived her. He insisted it was a mere optical illusion that misled her. Ruby clarified that her reaction to what she thought she saw had deeply hurt her best friend and her husband, who loved her even more intensely than in the first year of their marriage.

Regretting her impulsive reaction, Paula attempted to apologize to Dahlia, but she had disappeared and did not respond to any messages or letters.

A year later, Paula unexpectedly encountered her in the university corridors, in the company of an older man, a guest lecturer in the philosophy department. They appeared to be in love.

Dahlia introduced him as Magnus Van Doren, her philosophy professor and fiancé. She shared that they planned to leave the country in July, get married in Helsinki, and live in Magnus' home, where he taught at the local university. Magnus, who was twice divorced, had three grown children from his previous marriages.

Dahlia spoke to Paula with a distant coldness, her face etched with a strange, cool expression. Her smile was forced and did not reach her eyes. She relayed her news briefly, with neither joy nor excitement, as if she were a newscaster reporting to a stranger about the week's events.

Embarrassed, Paula congratulated the couple and tried to invite Dahlia to the cafeteria to apologize, explain... However, Dahlia quickly bid her farewell, without extending an invitation to her wedding or promising to stay in touch. True to her nature,

Dahlia had completely severed ties. Two decades later, Paula found her on Facebook, sent a friend request and a heartfelt private message. Dahlia accepted the friend request but did not respond to the heartfelt message.

The gnawing sensation of hunger compelled Paula to get up. Her discomfort intensified, not solely from the hunger. Her gaze fell on a couple embracing tightly on the nearby lawn, so engrossed in each other that the world around them seemed to vanish, leaving only them and their passion.

With a pang of nostalgia, Paula reminisced about how she and Ruby used to lose themselves in each other in their private Wuthering Heights in Hadar Carmel. She remembered their passionate tussles on the narrow bed in her childhood room and the nights that stretched until dawn in their modest two-room apartment in the student housing.

How had this emptiness taken hold inside her? How, with that long inventory checklist of all she had, did she feel such profound lack? What was missing? What was this old-new, unsettling sensation that felt like a cold splash of water unexpectedly poured over her? In her marriage, in the small family unit she had built and nurtured, she felt alone, utterly isolated.

It wasn't that she had stopped loving Ruby; the very mention of his name still sparked a warmth that made her rub her thighs together. She loved him unconditionally, desired him even more now than on the day she had first given in to him by the aqueduct in Caesarea. With each passing year, her love for him grew. She was losing herself, fading into the fabric of their absolute union.

Then why this overwhelming loneliness? Why this deep-seated emptiness? She was hungry, but not just for food. She craved Ruby's attention, his presence, more than anything.

She recalled that at this hour, he would be finishing his teaching assistant duties in the "Atomic Molecular Physics" course, intended for third-year undergraduates in physics.

Surely exhausted, he would have headed to the Mensa dining hall in the Natural Sciences building. Why had he stopped looking for her so they could have lunch together? Until two months ago, he had sought her out at every opportunity, wanting her company, pursuing her ardently. A poem by Dahlia Ravikovitch echoed in her ears:

An orange did love
The man who ate it.
A feast for the eyes
Is a fine repast;
Its heart held fast
His greedy gaze.

***

An orange, consumed
By the man who ate it,
Invaded his skin
To the flesh beneath.[3]

Was this what had happened to her? Had she been consumed by Ruby and become part of him? Lost within his flesh? This all-consuming relationship with Ruby was not nurturing her.

---

[3] Ravikovitch, Dahlia. "Love of a Golden Apple": ' Love of a Golden Apple', Sifriat Poalim, Published by HaKibbutz HaArtzi HaShomer HaTzair, 1976, p. 5

Was it real life or just fantasy

Where were these feelings of self-doubt, loneliness, and isolation coming from? Enough, she would not drown in self-pity on such a beautiful spring day. She refused to waste these two free hours brooding over dark thoughts. Ruby must be hungry too, and he was probably in the Mensa dining hall, waiting for her to join him for lunch. Just the two of them, without Don's interruptions.

She stood up from the grassy knoll, shook her hair that flowed past her waist, brushed off the blades of grass, grabbed her backpack, slipped her bare feet into her wooden clogs, and made her way to the Mensa. Pushing open the glass door, she was momentarily blinded by the sun rays streaming through the large windows overlooking the lawn. After her vision adjusted to the influx of light, she felt comforted once again by the abundance of warmth.

She saw Ruby's face, he was leaning over a table for two not far from where she stood. She raised her hand, almost calling out to him when she suddenly noticed he was dining with a young woman who looked barely eighteen, likely a student from the Pre-Enlistment Academic Program.

For a moment, she felt breathless as reality slipped from her grasp, her balance wavering. She tried to steady herself, grounding her feet, gripping reality firmly.

Her gaze returned to Ruby's table. The young woman sitting opposite him seemed vaguely familiar, yet she couldn't place her. He leaned towards the young woman, his hand resting on hers. Their eyes locked, heads almost touching, both laughing, appearing deeply connected and happy. Paula felt caught in her own trap, exposed to something that shamed her very existence.

She wanted to turn back, to flee, but before she could escape, Ruby looked up, and their eyes met.

His expression turned serious, and he quickly withdrew his hand from the young woman's. His face paled.

Then, recovering quickly, he waved cheerfully at Paula. A few seconds later, he added with a burst of feigned enthusiasm, "Hey, Paula, so glad you're here! Come join us, you've arrived just in time for the main course."

Paula trembled, struggling to control the surge of anger within her. Her entire body twisted in revulsion, pain shooting through parts of her she didn't even know could feel. Her body vehemently rejected the facade and deception she had just witnessed.

A cold sweat ran down her spine, as if trying to expel the crisis of trust she had endured. Instead of the healthy hunger she had felt moments earlier, she was overwhelmed with nausea, fighting the urge to vomit the bitter bile rising to her throat.

Taking a deep breath, she pushed the acid back down, determined not to let it embarrass her further. As she approached Ruby's table, she felt like she was intruding on the young pair's intimate moment, which had been blissful just seconds before.

"Fanny," Ruby said to the young woman, "Meet Paula, my beloved wife, the mother of my son. Paula, this is Fanny, my student in the reserve program. Come, take my seat. I'll grab another chair from nearby, and we can order the main course. I'm starving."

He quickly stood up, offering Paula his seat, helped her to sit down, and pulled another chair for himself from a nearby table. Paula tried to smile, but it came out distorted, her face twisting uncomfortably. Realizing her effort was futile, she resigned herself to seriousness.

Ruby went to fetch two plates of schnitzels, fries, and finely chopped salad. He also picked up two bottles of water and a chocolate mousse just for her, everything arranged on a single tray. As befitting a husband who knew his wife's desires well and was eager to fulfill them before she even voiced them.

Ruby decided on a tactical maneuver — a retreat from a tense situation. It was a sophisticated strategy for a calculated withdrawal, a moment to regroup. Fanny accompanied him to the counter to pick her main course. Left on the table were two deep, empty soup bowls, silent witnesses to a celebration that had started without her.

Paula was certain she recognized Fanny's face, but from where? When Fanny had extended her hand and chirped, "Pleased to meet you," Paula was sure she had heard that childish voice before.

She watched the counter where a long line had formed. Ruby and Fanny were engaged in intense conversation as they waited. Fanny looked upset, and Ruby seemed to be trying to calm her.

Why on earth did Paula feel guilty, as if she was the one intruding on their private paradise, disturbing the idyllic harmony that had existed just moments before? Ruby was her man. What was he doing with her? Why had he stopped looking for her to have lunch together? What were they sharing? What was the true nature of their relationship?

It was hard to believe that just a few days ago, they had been together in the most intimate way possible — *An orange, consumed by the man who ate it, invaded his skin to the flesh beneath.* With many reservations, she had revealed to him that she was pregnant again. She had hesitated to tell him about the pregnancy, wanting to be sure everything was in order.

That morning, they had planned to meet at the Moroccan restaurant in the nearby suburbs. After a romantic candlelit dinner, at midnight, they returned to their new home on Masada

Road. Don was sleeping at her parents'. She had prepared the bedroom in advance, laying their bed with satin sheets adorned with a black and white Chinese print. She scattered rose petals on the sheets and pillows, surrounded by candles in various colors and lavender incense, just as he liked. When the taxi arrived, she rushed up the stairs to their second-floor apartment, lighting the candles and incense, and turning on the record player.

Even in the taxi, after a few glasses of white wine at dinner, Ruby was in a romantic mood, and they clung to each other with the same old fervor from four years earlier. As he entered the bedroom, Lenny's voice, filled with desire, played in the background, "*Hold Me Tight.*" Paula wore a short, deep blue silk gown she had bought at Fanny Hill, a boutique specializing in erotic games and accessories. The boutique had been opened some time ago in the Old City by a returnee who wanted to bring European erotic modernism to their Negev Desert city.

Paula handed Ruby a glass of champagne, about to tell him she was pregnant. But before she could speak, Ruby passionately kissed her, enjoying her lips one at a time and then both together. He captured her tongue with his and forcefully refused to let go, dismissing all her attempts at negotiation. Paula knew that Ruby took no prisoners, and she was happy to submit to his touch, which stroked the length of her back through the delicate silk gown. His hand traveled down the backless gown to the base of her spine, where it slipped through the generous opening to cup her buttocks. First, he caressed them with a fluttering tenderness, then kneaded them firmly. The familiar thunder of galloping horses surged within her. Moans escaped from her lips, still pressed against his. Her hands stripped him of his shirt, and her erect nipples pierced his chest in an attempt to subdue him.

Ruby pulled her to him and laid her on the bed, their bodies intertwined, touching, kissing, and licking each other's most hidden spots. They were continuously wrapped in a modern dance that expressed a nearly violent intensity alongside fluttering softness.

His tongue tried to subdue her from behind her ear and up her neck, alternating between slow, gentle kisses and quick, biting ones — light yet intense, nearly driving her mad. His hand cupped her full breasts, and his tongue wrapped around her erect nipples, kissing, stroking, squeezing, and lightly biting. It was hard to tell who was leading the dance and who was being led. Sometimes he was on top, and sometimes she conquered his erect form, mounting him from above and trying to match her quivering body to his thrusts. In the end, they merged into one, their bodies intertwined in an ever-escalating rhythm — their rhythm, collapsing together at precisely the right time and place for both of them.

Afterwards, with her head resting on his shoulder and both of them still slick with sweat and breathing heavily, she told him he was going to be a father again, this time to a daughter, according to the ultrasound. She remembered how happy he had been, how they had fallen asleep contentedly in each other's arms.

Paula's gaze returned to the counter; the line had significantly shortened, and Ruby and Fanny were almost at the front. Then she remembered where she had seen Fanny. It was about four months earlier when they were still living in their small apartment in the student housing complex. One Monday, she had unexpectedly decided to skip her lectures and return home.

She wanted to use the day to prepare for a comprehensive literature exam, a challenging test covering two years' worth of material on modern and medieval prose and poetry, and literary theory.

Don was at daycare until five, and Ruby was teaching at the university, leaving her the entire apartment to herself.

Around one in the afternoon, when Ruby was supposed to be in his lab working on his research, she heard knocks at the door but chose to ignore them, not wanting to waste the precious hours she had carved out for herself. However, as the knocking grew more insistent, she tiptoed to the door and peered through the peephole. Standing outside was a slender young woman in a revealing purple crop top and tiny denim shorts, with frayed fringes dangling from the crotch and barely covering her buttocks. Her hair was dyed a bright orange and pulled up into a high ponytail. The young woman, otherwise unremarkable except for her vividly colored hair, continued to knock vigorously with her small fists, showing no signs of stopping.

As Paula debated whether to open the door to end the noise, which could potentially alarm the neighbors, she suddenly heard the young woman raise her squeaky voice, "Ruby, open the door, I know you're there. We agreed to meet..."

Without further thought or considering whether it was wise to confront the young woman, Paula opened the door and asked sternly, "Excuse me, can you immediately stop this racket? This is a family building, and there are babies sleeping at this hour."

The audacious young woman looked at Paula in astonishment and tried to push her way in while asking, "Isn't this Ruby's apartment? We had planned to meet here at noon..."

Paula blocked the door and said firmly, "Excuse me, could you not barge into my home? Who are you? What do you want? You must be one of the students he teaches. I don't understand why you're deluding yourself that my husband arranged to meet with you. I'm sure you're mistaken. Students aren't supposed to barge into their professors' homes. I ask you to leave immediately."

The young woman looked at Paula angrily, but her expression quickly shifted to a sly smile. "Really?" she said, "I didn't know Ruby was married. He promised to help me with my coursework. We arranged to meet at his place at noon, but maybe I was mistaken, and he meant for us to meet at the library or his lab… Well, goodbye then. Who would have thought Ruby was married," she muttered to herself. She slowly descended the stairs, giving Paula a look of mocking curiosity over her shoulder.

Paula stood dumbfounded at the doorway. Her study plans were ruined. Had she become the cliché? The lecturer's wife who his young admirers didn't know was married, allowing him to live out the fantasies of a sought-after bachelor?

About two hours later, Ruby came home, visibly distressed, and enveloped her in a wide embrace. "God, Paula. Why do you keep doing this to me? We had arranged to meet in the cafeteria for lunch. I waited there for an hour like an idiot, and guess who didn't show up? Please, stop being so irresponsible. You can't imagine what I went through. I searched for you all over the university. I was in the literature department, the philosophy department, the humanities Mensa, the social sciences building, everywhere. Finally, I decided to look for you at home. Good thing I found you. I was almost out of my mind…"

Paula looked at him, tears welling up in her eyes. She realized something was very wrong. Ruby was speaking faster and faster, avoiding her gaze. She could already detect his insincerity, his evasion of the truth. Any moment now, he would pull her close, press her head against his chest so she couldn't see the guilt in his eyes he knew she saw.

She pulled away from his grasp, maintained a safe distance, and struggled to breathe. She tried to organize her thoughts and calm her spirit, to suppress her anger and avoid letting Ruby escape into a violent argument or a reconciliatory sexual encounter.

She wanted to understand exactly what was going on, but deep down, she already knew. In truth, she had suspected for some time. There were signs, but she chose to ignore them, fearing to confront the truth, Ruby, and reality.

"Ruby, cut the act. You're humiliating both of us. Is this what our relationship has come to? You think I'm that stupid? After four years, this is how you honor me? Instead of showing exaggerated care and love..."

"Paula, what are you talking about? Did you forget we scheduled lunch together? I don't understand why you're pushing me away. What's all this anger about? Just because I care and miss you and want to eat with you? Is it that time of the month?" He ended his speech with a weak voice, trying a lame joke.

Paula felt herself losing control. She stepped closer and in an uncontrollable rage, she slapped him. Then she stepped back, screamed in fury, and lashed out at him verbally.

"And maybe you can explain why a young woman is knocking on our door, calling your name, surprised to find out I exist, that you are married and a family man, coming to meet you at our tiny dorm apartment that barely has room for a double bed and Don's bed? And all this effort just so you can 'help her study'? What exactly were you supposed to 'study' in such intimacy? Isn't the library meant for that? Perhaps the respected teaching assistant doesn't have an office where he can receive students? Oh, of course, it's inconvenient to 'study' in a university room because he shares it with another assistant, whose presence disrupts the 'studying'."

Ruby approached her, trying again to draw her close. His eyes pleaded with her to stop. "Come on, Paula. Stop, you can't be serious. Now I see what this anger is about. It must be Fanny. She's completely nuts. She's hitting on every teaching assistant in the department. Come on, did you see how she looks? What do you think I am, a pedophile? What do I have to do with such a disturbed young woman? Stop it with this nonsense."

"How did she know to come here on the day you thought I'd be at university lectures? I wasn't supposed to be home at all. You're insulting me with your ridiculous explanations. And how did she know where you live? It seems this wasn't her first time here. The only surprise was that she didn't know you have a family. Do me a favor, don't turn me into a cliché — the wife of a young lecturer looking for excitement with his students."

Paula grabbed her bag, pushed past Ruby, who was blocking the door, and ran out, trying to hide her tear-stained face. She didn't want him to see the disappointment and humiliation she felt. After four years, she had become just another laughable statistic.

Feeling nauseated again, she saw Ruby and Fanny approaching the cash register. Any moment now, they would join her, and she would have to deal with all the lies, the pretense, and the deceit.

So, Fanny was still at the university. Alive, kicking, and very much entangled in Ruby's life. Paula struggled to understand how he could lead such a double life, especially after their intense nights together and his expressed joy about the new addition to their family. How could he risk everything?

After that argument, she left home with Don and spent two weeks at her parents' house. Ruby repeatedly came knocking on their door, tried to talk to her, pleaded to explain, but she ignored all his attempts. Even at the university, when he ambushed her as she left lecture halls or the library, she refused to listen to his pleas.

Eventually, after two weeks in which Don cried incessantly, begging to see his father, she relented and agreed to go out for coffee with Ruby. He reiterated that Fanny was just his student, nothing more. Just a strange and troubled young woman known around the university for clinging to every young lecturer in the department.

"You can check with Judah and Raffi, they both have families like me. She did the exact same thing to them."

Ruby told her he had complained about Fanny to the university's disciplinary committee, and since she was reprimanded, she vanished and stopped appearing in his classes. He believed she had left the university.

I need to get out of here, Paula thought, *in a moment, they will sit next to me, and I can't deal with them right now*. She tore a piece of paper from her notepad and hastily scribbled a few words: "*I need to pick up Don from daycare. See you at home.* **Bon Appétit!!!**" Grabbing her bag, she fled as fast as she could.

From the corner of her eye, she caught the shocked expression on their faces as they walked in perfect harmony, trays in hand, towards her table.

Was it real life or just fantasy

34

Pnina Tel Dan

Menachem

The obituaries that Menachem Sheldon followed so religiously ignited a spark of interest in his life. Without them, his life would have been dreary, leaving no lasting impact. To maintain a symmetry in the predictable world he inhabited, he, too, left no mark on it.

The only event that left a deep impression and shaped his life was the death of his father. His father passed away in his mid-forties, precisely one week after Menachem celebrated his bar mitzvah at the Great Synagogue in Jerusalem. Menachem recited the *Parshat "Tazria-Metzora"*, a portion from Leviticus focusing on laws of ritual purity, childbirth, and skin diseases, before a congregation largely comprised of strangers. They watched him with boredom, eagerly awaiting the end of his recitation so they could enjoy the raisin lekach cake, poppy and cinnamon cookies, and salted fish that his parents had lavishly spread on the long tables along with vodka, arak, wine, and juices. The aroma of soused herring, kippers, and salmon captivated the worshippers far more than the timid, nervous mumblings of the thirteen-year-old confronting the open Torah scroll.

After Menachem finished reciting the *haftarah* — a series of selections from the books of the Prophets (Nevi'im) that are read in synagogue services on Sabbaths, festivals, and fast days, typically following the Torah reading — he thanked his parents in his bar mitzvah speech for his upbringing. The children and women began pelting him with vibrant candies and almonds encased in a hard, colorful coating. A covert competition emerged among the children to see who could hit Menachem's head the most. Despite his efforts to dodge, their malicious throws inevitably hit him, extracting cries of pain and eliciting peals of laughter from the children and smiles from their mothers. Following the monotonous Torah reading, everyone indulged in a moment of bliss, a Sabbath delight.

The week his father died, during which the Torah portion known as "Acharei Mot" (meaning "after the death of") was read, marked a pivotal moment in Menachem's life. This section of Leviticus, which begins with rituals performed after the death of Aaron's sons and includes laws about the Day of Atonement, seemed eerily fitting. Almost joyful during the *shivah* — the seven-day Jewish mourning period — Menachem and his mother were no longer alone. Visitors came to their home, lavishing attention upon them, their words wrapping the bereaved in the warmth of an embroidered silk scarf, whose beauty and pleasantness made up for its impracticality. As they engaged in rituals of grief and remembrance, their days became more focused, as if someone swept away the dust of their misery and replaced it with a life of prosperous dignity.

Throughout that week, they were surrounded by people, most of whom Menachem met for the first time during the shivah. They shared stories of his father Berko's youth, his military service, and how he met Menachem's mother Rachel, whom they called Ruha. His parents met in the Kfar Hayarok boarding school. Berko, two years younger than Ruha, worshipped the ground she walked on. They were both brought to the Kfar Hayarok as part of the Youth Aliyah from Bulgaria, smoldering embers rescued from the ashes of the Holocaust. He was a skeletal figure with a large head and piercing yellowish-green eyes; she was sturdy, her abundant hair golden like ripe wheat. They first met at dawn during milking and never parted thereafter, keeping to themselves and not mingling with others in the village.

Even though the mourners clearly exaggerated their praise of Berko out of customary respect — since during the week of *Acharei Mot*, it was improper to speak ill of the deceased — Menachem didn't mind. He eagerly absorbed their words, even when they veered into exaggerated anecdotes about their own lives, and those of their friends, and how they had met his father.

Ruha, his widowed mother, a hollowed-out, bitter woman in her mid-forties, seemed almost radiantly happy among the people who showered attention upon her and her son, instilling in them, albeit briefly, an illusion of life. After the mourning period, mother and son reverted to their predictable, desolate existence, drained of any vestige of vitality.

Eventually, in her late sixties, overwhelmed by grief and illness, she freed her son and the world of her presence.

Without a single soul left in his dreary life, Menachem felt the weight of his isolation. His body was covered with painful, inflamed psoriatic scales. His skin craved the warmth of a touch. Considering adopting a cat, his asthma condemned him to a solitary existence. He lived in Kiryat Hayovel in Jerusalem, in his parents' apartment, where he had spent his entire life.

He barely made ends meet, living almost entirely in solitude in a modest, nondescript workers' housing complex built in the fifties. The fish swimming in the living room aquarium were his only companions.

Menachem was of average height, his complexion faded, his hair frizzy in shades of grayish-flax, and his skin yellowish. His skin's texture, reminiscent of ancient parchments coated with candle wax, allowed him to blend almost completely with the ancient books on the shelves of the National Library where he worked. His eyes, large and deep, sparkled with a potent greenish-yellow hue, similar to his father's before him.

After his father's death, Menachem harbored an intense longing for the familial warmth he remembered from the shiva. Throughout his life, he sought to reignite this experience time and again.

Following his mother's death, when he was in his early forties, Menachem, a certified librarian at the reference desk of the National Library, began to fervently follow obituaries in the newspaper. He carefully selected a few notices each week, attending the shiva of people he did not know, sometimes even more than once.

His life revolved around these families who opened their homes to him. They shared their grief, exposing him to the intimate moments of their lives. Sitting, listening, and nodding, his eyes shone with interest. Once he had gleaned the life secrets of the deceased and their families, he would contribute, with heartfelt empathy, one or two episodes in which the deceased featured as his friend and companion, whether as a co-worker, a childhood friend, in a youth movement, the army, or on a global adventure — stories he adopted for himself and realized only in his tangled imagination.

Those who saw Menachem at these condolence gatherings would not recognize the normally unremarkable librarian from the National Library. On one particular Tuesday, while perusing the obituaries in *Haaretz*, one notice stirred significant excitement within him:

"We mourn the untimely death of Nathan Shemesh, beloved husband, father, and devoted friend. The family sits shiva at 8 Aharonov Street, Beit Hakerem."

Deciding to leave his shift at the reference desk early that day, Menachem excused his premature departure at two o'clock to his supervisors, citing unforeseen personal reasons. After leaving his post, he hurried to Shimon, the barber from the Mahaneh Yehudah Market, for his usual full care package: a haircut, shave, trimming of ear, eyebrow, and nostril hair, a manicure, and a face and scalp massage with hot towels.

From there, Menachem hurried to Kirschenbaum's store and bought, wholesale, some of his finest buttoned shirts and several matching pairs of pants typically purchased for grooms. After also acquiring two buttoned jackets — one light, the other dark blue — he picked out silk ties in matching colors and quickly moved on to Rabinovich's shoe store. There, he bought two pairs of soft moccasins, one light, the other dark. He also added several pairs of Egyptian cotton socks and high-quality underwear.

That very evening, at six o'clock, he entered the house of the Shemesh family and stepped into their elegantly designed drawing room. In the large room, at the center of a low Natuzzi sofa upholstered in lilac velvet, sat the widow Chaya Shemesh, nestled in her children's embrace. Just as her Hebrew last name suggested, she had been the sunshine of Menachem's life during his library science studies at the Hebrew University. Menachem means comforting or consoling, and as his own first name suggested, he had arrived to console her.

She remained as beautiful and radiant as he had remembered from twenty years earlier. Slightly fuller now, her face bore fine, soft lines that added a touch of grace to her expression. She wiped away tears that streaked her face, and Menachem observed that, despite her grief, the light still shone in her clear blue eyes.

Menachem sat quietly, trying to make himself small, yet unable to take his eyes off her. Uncharacteristically, he didn't engage in the conversations or pretend to be an acquaintance of the deceased. Noticing that Chaya felt unwell before the prayer, he did not join the other men but stayed by the widow's side, offering her a glass of water to refresh her.

On the second day, he sat by her side in silence, loyal and devoted, groomed and quite striking in his meticulous attire; he helped by bringing her drinks, listened attentively to her stories about her husband, and responded with polite, empathetic nods to every word she spoke.

Each night during the shiva, he eagerly awaited the next morning, the right moment when he could reenter Chaya's life and sit beside her. He no longer felt as ostracized as he had during his bar mitzvah when he read *Parshat Tazria-Metzora*. Menachem had become a significant presence in Chaya's eyes, and she increasingly relied on the small services he specially provided for her.

Every morning, he rose with the "*Shehecheyanu*" blessing on his lips to express his gratitude, grateful to know that Chaya Shemesh, the secret love of his youthful days, still illuminated the gloomy darkness of his faded emotions. Chaya had been a stunningly beautiful student during his time at the library science school. He had fallen in love with her the moment he saw her during a lesson on the Dewey Decimal System. The decimal system had been challenging for Chaya, and Menachem volunteered to help her with class exercises and study for the final exam. She was kind and appreciative of his help, but truthfully, beyond their academic collaboration, she knew nothing — and preferred not to know anything — about his existence.

Now, sitting across from her as she mourned her beloved husband Nathan, who had been shot during a reserve duty incident in the territories where he commanded his company, Menachem felt a sense of hope tinged with promise for the first time in his life. He was almost as happy as he had been during the first shiva of his childhood.

By the fourth day, the flow of condoling visitors had dwindled, and Menachem, sitting like a family member by the widow's side, served her faithfully with a keen ear and supportive shoulder. Chaya grew accustomed to having him by her side, and he became an inseparable part of her environment. She had not yet fully realized the magnitude of her loss, but in the well-groomed Menachem, she found a glimmer of hope for the future.

At the end of the week, Menachem informed his workplace that due to a death in the family, he would not be able to come to work the following week. Much to the dismay of Chaya's children and relatives, Menachem began showing up at her home early in the morning.

Chaya welcomed his visits and publicly thanked him for his help and for his presence in her home. He had officially become a constant figure in her life, and gradually, hesitantly, with a quiet yet confident voice, he began to share more about himself.

Chaya remembered their acquaintance from her library science school days and the many hours he had dedicated to helping her prepare for exams.

Now, they had become soulmates, as they discovered they were old acquaintances of twenty years. "It's quite a slice of common history that we share," Chaya explained to her sister-in-law and to her two energetic teenage daughters, Rinat and Sarit, fourteen-year-old twins who were her spitting image.

Menachem continued to visit Chaya's home every morning even after the shiva week had ended. He listened to her reminisce about her life with her husband, her yearnings, and her longings. He wiped away her tears and took care of every need she had. Each evening, he would leave her and return to the cold emptiness of his own apartment.

Even after returning to work in the third week after Nathan's death, Menachem maintained a strong connection with Chaya, helping her with all the bureaucratic aspects of settling the estate, the unveiling of the headstone, debt payments, and household management.

"Menachem, I have an unusual request for you. I have already taken advantage of your . . . generosity so much. . . it makes me a bit uncomfortable to ask this."

"Stop, Chaya, you know how much I enjoy your company. I feel vital when I can help you. When someone . . .when you. . . need me, and I can alleviate, even slightly, the burdens of your life, it makes me feel grateful to be a note within your life's melody."

"Still, the girls and my sister-in-law say I'm taking advantage of you, and that I will eventually have to pay the price for it. They worry you'll grow tired of me."

"Really, Chaya, how could you be taking advantage of someone who is willingly responsive to your needs and enjoys being around you? For me, these are mere trifles, minor tasks that I am trusted with. But with you, it's different. Nathan was the one who always took care of such matters."

"True, you're right, but this time it is different. The request is somewhat more intimate. I must remove all of Nathan's clothes and belongings from the house. I know it has only been three months, but the sights, the smells, and the memories have become simply unbearable."

"Do you want me to clear out his belongings? And what should I do with them?"

"I prefer that you give them to those in need who might use them, perhaps to some charity organization. I would not wish to see them worn by anyone I know. I don't know why, but this task is impossible for me. Too painful. I would prefer if you handled it. I will understand if you refuse, if it's too much of a burden."

"Chaya, all you need to do is ask. You know that. I would give you both halves of my kingdom."

Menachem's yellowish eyes smiled at his beloved in an attempt to mask the jealousy he felt over her pain and deep longing for her deceased husband.

The following week, on Sunday, Chaya went with her daughters to stay with a family member, saying she would remain there until the next evening. She entrusted Menachem with the house keys and dozens of large black plastic bags, pleading with him in trembling anxiety to clear out her late husband's belongings.

Menachem entered her meticulously kept house as though stepping into a holy sanctuary. Upon entering, he removed his shoes, shed his clothes, and donned a white robe he customarily wore on Shabbat.

This was the first time he had seen her bedroom, a spacious, brightly lit room. At its center stood a cream-colored canopy bed draped with bluish covers. The walls displayed reproductions of paintings of women by Renoir, Matisse, and Klimt. The massive double Bauhaus-style windows were dressed in cream-colored curtains embroidered with blue forget-me-not flowers. The matching-colored carpet created an atmosphere of tranquility, warmth, and a harmonious abundance. Walk-in closets flanked the bedroom, hers on the right, his on the left.

Before starting his task, Menachem removed the bed cover and lay down where Chaya's purple nightgown rested. He placed his head on her pillow, embraced the silky fabric, and inhaled her scent. Then he played some quiet music on his iPhone.

Chaya had left her daughters with her relative and returned home. She entered the bedroom without a word, peeled off her white organza dress, under which her glowing skin highlighted her curves. Menachem extended his arms toward her, and she lay beside him, her sensuous lips tracing his body. Her gentle kisses gradually became wilder, more urgent, covering his skin with increasing ardor. His body began to tremble, until a damp warmth awakened him from his delightful illusion. In moments, he realized that, as usual, he was living on borrowed time — a life that, in some alternate universe, would have seen Chaya as his wife, his love, sharing not just his bed but his entire life.

Come evening, after preparing some sandwiches and drinking a cup of strong Turkish coffee, he began to pack the closet's contents into the large bags. Giorgio Armani suits, semi-elegant sports jackets, luxurious buttoned shirts, Valentino

Garavani and Gucci shoes, and branded sportswear. A seemingly endless abundance of a man upon whom fortune had once smiled, until suddenly it did not.

One of the upper shelves held branded silk ties, cufflinks, and gold Rolex watches, and was twice as thick as the other shelves. After clearing its contents, Menachem noticed a protruding button at the edge of the shelf. He pressed it, releasing a hidden drawer. Inside, he found a thick, white plastic card. Lifting it revealed a flash drive. He rushed to the living room, placed his bag by the door, and, without a second thought, slipped the plastic card into it.

He then redoubled his efforts, and within an hour, he had packed the entire room's contents into the bags. He loaded them into his car's trunk, returned to the house, quickly dressed, tidied Nathan's bedroom and walk-in closet, washed the dishes, and left the apartment as clean, aired, and immaculate as he had found it.

Without stopping to think, he drove to the local community donations center, dropped off the bags as an anonymous donation, and hurried back to his apartment.

During this time, he completely forgot about Nathan's card and flash drive, which lay in his bag alongside some gold valuables. Later, back at home, he decided to keep them safe and consult with Chaya about what to do with them.

That evening, he retrieved the card with the flash drive and inserted it into his computer. Images popped up on the screen showing Nathan at wild parties with young women. The dates on the photos and the correspondence, which appeared to have been deleted from Nathan's computer and saved here, made it clear that Nathan had led a fervent and active life of sex and love outside his marriage. During his business trips to Silicon Valley in the US and Taiwan, where his high-tech company had branches, he lived as a sought-after bachelor, enjoying the best the world had to offer.

Menachem felt relieved. Chaya would finally stop glorifying Nathan to him. She would stop reminiscing about her perfect marriage and the unconditional love her "perfect, faithful" husband had lavished on her.

Now, he would no longer be just a shoulder for her to cry on. She would see him, Menachem, not just as an alternative partner responsible only for bureaucratic tasks or as the perfect guide for managing her financial affairs. Up until now, he had been burdened with responsibilities without any privileges. Chaya had never showered him with unconditional love.

Even in the misery of his own modest apartment, the scent of her nightgown clung to his skin — the scent of musk, reminiscent of the oil the High Priest would apply to the sacrifices before offering them to God.

Menachem envisioned moving in with Chaya, sharing family meals with her and her daughters. His body ached for the touch of her ample figure. He felt his manhood stir at the absence of her presence.

Once Chaya confronted her husband's betrayal, his debauched life, and the money he had squandered on other women, she would surely come to her senses and stop pining for him. Instead, she would see him, Menachem. He would no longer be a temporary fill-in, exploited as during their university days.

They would live as a couple, perhaps even marry. He would have his own family. He would adopt the girls and finally belong. They would take family trips in Israel and abroad. He would be happy. She would learn to appreciate his love and devotion. Who knew, maybe one day, she might even learn to love him.

Menachem considered sending her the pictures he had printed from the flash drive anonymously by courier. He planned to include a letter explaining, in unequivocal terms, the kind of immoral villain her husband had been. Menachem wrote the letter in English and signed it under the name of a friend who was supposedly aware of her husband's double life. He decided to schedule a FedEx delivery for the envelope to reach Chaya first thing the next morning.

When the girls left for school, Menachem and Chaya sat in the kitchen sharing a pleasant conversation over an intimate breakfast for two. The doorbell rang, prompting Chaya to answer the front door, and she returned holding a brown envelope.

Before Menachem could warn her, the letter and pictures slid out. She looked at the pictures in confusion, and her expression slowly shifted to one of shock and disgust. Finally, she opened the letter and began to read it quietly; her face grew even more troubled and contorted with distress.

She looked up at Menachem, her eyes clouded with pain, struggling in vain to articulate her thoughts. Her mouth opened as if gasping for air. Menachem could have sworn he saw bubbles of water and air escaping it. Despite her efforts, no sound came out.

She looked as if a sledgehammer had struck her skull, unwilling to fully absorb the harsh reality before her. She closed her eyes and withdrew into herself. After long minutes of silence, she opened them, and Menachem realized that to her, he had ceased to exist. Now, she seemed even more pathetic than him. More isolated. Made grotesque by her adoration for a husband who had misled her. Her indifferent gaze passed right through him. He would never be more than a reliable household helper to her, a family friend who could be trusted.

He understood that his role had ended. He could no longer revive her love for her husband through his empathetic listening to her stories. He had gained nothing from exposing her husband's double life. On the contrary, they both ended up losing.

The chime of the alarm clock he had set in anticipation of the courier's arrival jolted Menachem awake. He vividly recalled the dream in which Chaya received his FedEx letter, and how, with the opening of an envelope, her life's illusions were shattered by his own hand.

Like a mantra, he repeated the insight from his dream: he would gain nothing from Chaya knowing the truth about her husband. If he could not continue to serve as a mirror reflecting her past happiness, she would, he was certain, sever all ties with him. She would not be able to face him knowing that everything she had shared with him about her life with Nathan was a web of lies. She would be unable to deal with the humiliation.

Menachem's body retreated back into its former void. The colors of his hopes faded as before, and he rose slowly, feeling completely powerless yet resolutely determined. He burned the letter and the pictures, removed the card with the flash drive from the computer, and threw it into the vast new aquarium that dominated his living room.

The flash drive sank amid his dreams and hopes, resting among corals, goldfish, and tilapias in all the colors of the rainbow. It was the perfect final resting place for Nathan's secrets and Menachem's silent loyalty. Here, he would forever shield the threat to the illusion of Chaya's perfect marriage.

Pnina Tel Dan

Broken

Summer 1970. A group of teens — boys and girls —create a living sculpture of vibrant youth on the stone structure at the center of Sahne National Park. The area is lush with greenery, dotted with rivulets and tree-shaded waterfalls. The air is humid and thick, sunlit. All are huddled together, laughing, gazing at the camera. They are all seventeen or eighteen years old — except for Tamara. Standing in the center of the photo, twelve-year-old Tamara has yet to grow into her teenage years. She's their mascot, her gaze drifting almost beyond the edge of the frame. She notices Uzi, the one fracturing the group's harmony, chipping away at the illusion of flawless youth. He stands atop the shattered parts of the sculpture, clinging with one hand, distanced from the others. His face is strained into a semblance of a smile, his eyes filled with vulnerability and disappointment. Tamara remembers hearing from Dalit on the way to the park that Uzi and Nira had split up.

Uzi and Nira had been a constant pair since they were about thirteen, from the time the group formed. Tamara had met the group — children of Eastern European immigrants — during her summer vacations. She spent almost every summer at her Aunt

Sarah's in Caesarea before the city was divided into upscale villas and a development town. Back then, everyone mingled freely. The older kids had her run errands, affectionately calling her "Gofer." The girls enjoyed combing her hair, acting as big sisters, openly discussing their relationships with the boys next to her. They all had steady boyfriends: Dalit with Dudu, Rimona with Shimon, Noah with Hana, and, of course, Uzi with Nira.

One summer evening, most of the group, boys and girls, sat on the grass, listening to music and chatting. Uzi arrived on his bike and joined them. An older man with a tired, unkempt appearance, wearing stained blue work coveralls, staggered toward them, dragging his bicycle. He bellowed, "Uzi, Uzi, where are you? Your mom's looking for you. Get back home immediately, she's sick again, making my life miserable, and it's killing me." Tamara saw Uzi's face blanch, his eyes flickering as he struggled to suppress his tears of humiliation. Abruptly, he stood, kicked his bike in anger, smashing it against a eucalyptus tree trunk, and ran off.

Rimona later explained that Uzi's father, perpetually drunk, continuously quarreled with Veronika, his wife. Uzi's mother, a woman plagued by depression and jealousy, fantasized about non-existent affairs of her husband, forever darkening his days.

Uzi had scarcely spent time at home since he began dating Nira, a girl whose poised and graceful demeanor revealed her as a talented ballet dancer. Nira, who lived in the white house across the street, had met Uzi at school. A handsome youth, with black hair and eyes, he was also an outstanding athlete. Nira's mother, a dentist, was close to Uzi's struggling family and supported the young couple's relationship. She took pity on Uzi and offered him a room in her house. Everyone believed Uzi and Nira were inseparable. Until that trip to Sahne Park, they were almost considered engaged. Rimona added that Nira's older sister, Rachel, introduced Nira to a young man, a recent immigrant from Moscow and an orthopedist, whom she felt was more suitable for Nira and their family.

On Fridays, everyone — now married with children — continued to meet regularly. Uzi, however, always arrived alone, introspective and detached from the familial bonds forming before him.

At one of these Friday gatherings, Uzi arrived with Noa, a young, tall, melancholic woman he had met during his time at the Wingate Institute. Tamara thought that although the couple arrived together, it was their shared solitude, both individual and collective, that united them. Eventually, the pair married, but they never had children.

On a sunny winter afternoon in 2014, in the well-tended garden of Dalit and Dudu's home in Hadera, the group gathered around tables brimming with food. The men, their hair flecked with white, some desperately trying to conceal their bulging bellies beneath too-tight jeans. The women, whose hair color had surely changed but maintained meticulously by their stylists, had lost some of their youthful agility, their energetic spirit replaced by a serene contentment.

The group, whose members had drifted apart over the years, had reconnected through WhatsApp and decided to reunite and catch up. Most now had grandchildren. Photos were shared, stories recounted, and, at the end of the meeting, it was time for a group photo. Tamara volunteered to take the picture. Through the camera lens, a close-knit group of cheerful elderlies was captured, smiling straight at the iPhone camera, comfortably seated on the plastic chairs in the garden. Off to the side, slightly apart from the others, almost out of the frame beside his broken chair, stood Uzi — a lean, divorced man, his once handsome face now gaunt, his dark eyes fixed on Nira as she embraced Alexei, her husband.

Pnina Tel Dan

Meeting, Hardly Meeting[4]

Alarming sounds tore at my eardrums. Something sticky trickled down my chin. I lifted my head from the keyboard, where I had collapsed a couple of hours earlier. The clock at the corner of the screen read 23:30. The display was filled with line after line of: *"I have nothing to write, I have nothing to writeeeeeee..."*

An incoming message sliced through the small email window. An invite for a Zoom conversation from Yosi Zigenboim. "My brother has completely lost it," I muttered discontentedly to myself, "what's so urgent in the middle of the night?"

Driven by the corona-induced madness and horrific scenarios, I reluctantly agreed to take the call. But not before ensuring that my camera was off. The imprint of the keyboard keys on my right cheek, the tracks of dried, sticky saliva smeared over the Sahara-like expanse that was once my face — all of it made for a decidedly unappealing sight.

---

[4] This is also the name of a famous Hebrew poem by the poetess "Rachel." © Translation: 1994, Jean Shapiro Cantu. Robert Friend
From: *Flowers of Perhaps: Selected Poems of Rachel*
Publisher: Menard, London, 1994

Yosi barged into my room and, true to form, without any unnecessary pleasantries, blurted out, "Awake, huh? Can't sleep? How was the Passover Seder? What are you doing? You know your camera's off, right? Turn it on, sis, let's see the damage."

"The camera's busted," I lied boldly. "I'm fine. The Seder was no different from any other year, except that it was on Zoom. Just another chaotic family gathering. And how's your Slu... I mean, your Sarah?" I caught the Freudian slip just in time.

"Ha! Sarah organized a proper religious Seder. She got instructions from the community Rabbi in Barcelona. We're also under lockdown, so we joined in with the kids on Zoom. She really went all out, adhered to every detail. Hard to believe my *shiksa* has turned into a full-fledged kosher Rebbetzin. So, what were you doing at the computer? Finally getting back to that novel?"

"I've signed up for an online writing course. Trying to tackle an assignment. The plot revolves around a secret. I'm meant to write 'about it' without revealing 'it'," I quoted the guidelines I'd received. "I need to convey messages in a monologue. Reveal just a bit, and weave the rest into the subtext."

"Oh, speaking of secrets, guess who called me? Kora, Shimon's wife. Remember Shimon?"

"Shimon... Of course, I remember him. How could I forget? How's he doing?"

The memory jolted me back to the scorching summer of '72 in Beersheba. I had just turned fifteen. It was my last summer before high school. The first time I was supposed to travel alone to Haifa for my summer vacation. My cousin Tamara had invited me to stay with her young, hip family.

With my parents at work, I had the whole house to myself. Yosi was playing cards with the gang at Shimon's place, as they did every Wednesday.

And there I was, in shorts and an old-man-style black undershirt, dancing to the Beatles' "Yellow Submarine," with the brown suitcase open and clothes strewn all around, trying to decide what to pack for the trip, dreaming up vacation plans...

The door, usually unlocked, suddenly swung open, and all six feet and some of Shimon filled the gap. His face, slightly flushed, bore his usual goofy grin. Dripping with sweat, he collapsed into his typical antics on the sofa...

"Waaater, waaater, my Fatma," he attempted to conjure a throaty Arabic accent from his Romanian roots.

"Okay, ya *Rais*, ya *tawil*," I responded, playfully using Arabic terms that roughly translated to 'chief' and 'tall one', "where did you park your camel? It must be as thirsty as you."

I handed him a bottle of cold water. He couldn't wait for me to pour it into a glass and drank straight from the bottle.

He obviously acted the wild man to mask his embarrassment, trying to lighten the mood. Shimon was my brother's best friend. They were part of a tight-knit group of about ten youths, boys and girls around eighteen, living it up during their summer vacation before military draft, having known each other since elementary school.

I was the group's "tag-along", younger than the others. My brother tolerated my presence in silence because I served as his fig leaf. Having me there meant he had free rein to do as he pleased. Our parents were delighted that we got along splendidly and that someone was looking out for me. We had a tacit agreement: whatever happened in Shimon's apartment stayed in Shimon's apartment.

Shimon was the only child of parents who had emigrated from Romania, survived the horrors of the Holocaust, lost their families, and united to nurture the last scion of their lineage. They owned the neighborhood butcher shop, purchased with the reparations money received from Germany. They were decent, hardworking people who shrewdly invested their earnings in real estate.

Shimon was the only one among us who received, for his eighteenth birthday, a three-room apartment and a secondhand Ford from his parents. He painted the car a bright lemon yellow and decorated it with remarkable gangster flair in flashy accessories. It was aptly nicknamed the "Yellow Submarine."

Shimon's apartment served as the gang's lair. There, they gathered every evening to chat, argue, smoke cigarettes and joints, and play poker on Wednesdays. They danced to the tunes of Pink Floyd, Rare Earth, The Beatles, Leonard Cohen, King Crimson, and Janis Joplin. Couples would retreat to the rooms, navigating the complicated, stuttering pathways of young romance.

The apartment also had an old black-and-white Siemens television, which I had claimed for myself. During their Friday parties, I would devoutly watch Egyptian romance films on it, crying over the characters' tragic fates, warming to the lovers' kisses, and trying to match the belly dancers at the local haflas.

Shimon would often join in on my belly dancing. He'd place an upturned pot on his head, wrap a scarf around his waist, shove a cigarette between his lips, and never forget to dramatically whisk away the red tablecloth with its long golden tassels, like a magician. He'd wrap it around my waist, his huge hands spread wide, clapping wildly while shouting at the top of his lungs, "Yalla, yalla, ya Fatma, show them what Hungarian belly dancing is all about!"

Shimon and I always had our little inside jokes, our shared craziness, but he never came just to see me. It was always with the rest of the gang.

I wasn't really part of the gang, so I was a little amazed to see him there on the day he knew Yosi was out playing poker with the others at their usual meeting place.

But what am I rambling about? I knew we had a good rapport. We always laughed, gossiped about everyone and everything. But the age difference and his status as my brother's best friend rendered him invisible in all other respects. Yet, I knew I was headed for trouble — nothing good could come from this eerie visit.

"Yosi said you're going to Haifa all by yourself. Our little squirt has grown up…"

Shimon spoke, and I wasn't sure if he was talking to me or at me. He was all hand gestures, flushed and dripping with sweat. Ever since I'd known him, he had always been sweaty, but this was excessive even for him. Only occasional words pierced the dense white silence and the muddled, mushy fog filling my mind. Sweat droplets slid across his forehead, dampening his face. One droplet, with acrobatic precision, hung from his nose and, miraculously, stayed there. I saw him get animated, blush, and wipe his sweaty hands on his jeans. He laughed in his sweat-soaked shirt, shook his head, somewhat jittery, a dancer performing to the sound of a Yemenite tin drum.

A fly entered the room, buzzing around, occasionally landing on different parts of Shimon's body, mostly on his sweaty face. All our lighthearted banter and silliness evaporated in the oppressive heat. He continued speaking with a forced cheerfulness, clearly afraid to stop and succumb to embarrassment. Occasionally, the word "Haifa" penetrated my thoughts, but nothing more. It was as if I had gone deaf. I couldn't decode the white noise and make sense of the words.

My thoughts were constantly interrupted by what to pack. Whether to take my red bikini or just settle for the turquoise one-piece that highlighted the color of my eyes and other newly discovered curves from that summer.

I was thrilled about my visit to Haifa. My cousin and her husband were a wonderful couple. He was an interior designer and painter, a graduate of the Bezalel Academy of Arts, a tanned, muscular, and exotic version of Apollo, as my aunt described him.

Tamara had promised to introduce me to his younger brother, who was just as hot. Tamara and her husband were part of a free-spirited group of artists, actors, and painters who savored life and flouted conventions. She promised me days at the beach, movies, theater shows, parties, and coffee house gatherings with their friends.

Occasionally, I smiled and nodded at Shimon, which he might have taken as agreement to everything he was saying. After a few seemingly eternal minutes, he finally mentioned that the others were expecting him back at the lair and melted back into the heat.

It proved to be unforgettable summer. Never in my wildest dreams did I imagine that in my short life, I'd witness and experience so many thrilling things. I met interesting and exceptional people. Tamara kept her word and introduced me to Dave, her husband Alon's younger and hunky brother. I lived up to all my expectations, experienced my first kiss, and even fell in love, which flared up quickly and faded just as fast towards the end of my vacation in Haifa, without any major dramas or regrets.

Unfortunately, my mother insisted I return home two weeks before the vacation ended, and I had to settle back into the dusty reality of a Beersheba summer.

To cheer me up and dissolve any opposition from my parents, my brother took me to Shimon's army recruitment party. It was the last summer celebration for the entire gang before their draft.

Shimon was his usual playful self, joking and frolicking with everyone. He danced with a pretty, somewhat plump blonde girl and embraced her. Later, I learned she was Kora, a girl he had met after returning from Haifa when he went to his optometrist to repair his broken glasses. She was the optometrist's daughter, helping out in the shop during her summer break.

I learned all this later at the party when my brother, Yosi, decided to introduce me to Kora and explain how she and Shimon had met. Shimon ignored me throughout the party, and when I wished him well on his upcoming service, he turned away rudely, ignoring me completely. I didn't let it go, and at the first opportunity, I pulled him aside into the kitchen and confronted him. I opened my mouth and let him have it: "Can you explain, *ya Rais*, why the cold shoulder? Did I do something to offend you?"

"Why did you stand me up? We agreed to meet at 'Palace' to watch 'Gone with the Wind', *ya Fatma*. Is this how they taught you to treat your *Rais*?" he attempted to joke weakly.

"Ahhh... I... I had to look after my nephew Maor. He was ill and his parents had to go to work. I had no way of letting you know. I'm so sorry."

I lied through my teeth. I didn't have the heart to admit that due to my attention-deficit disorder, I hadn't heard a word he'd said that day.

"Never mind, Fatma. I've already replaced you with a more sophisticated blonde upgrade. So, it's all good," he said, his smile tinged with bitterness.

After that, I hadn't heard from him in years. He didn't attend my wedding or my son's brit-milah. I had invited him to both — the wedding and the sacred circumcision ceremony that welcomes newborn Jewish boys into the covenant. His absence was felt keenly at these milestones.

While studying for my BA at Ben-Gurion University, I encountered him in the humanities library. He spoke to me coolly, almost ignoring me. Later, it struck me as odd that I had run into him there, as he was studying mechanical engineering in a building much further away.

A few years later, Ruthie, my best friend and soul mate, told me that everyone was surprised by my absence at Shimon's wedding. I felt hurt. Insulted. I didn't tell her that Shimon hadn't even sent me an invitation.

Now, Yosi was trying to tell me something, but once again the white noise and mushy mental fog in my brain blocked out what was being transmitted online from far-off Barcelona.

"Ella, are you l i s t e n i n g, or have you drifted off to your parallel dimension again?"

"I hear you. You said Kora called."

"I told you that fifteen minutes ago. You're incorrigible, letting me talk to myself," he grumbled.

"Enough with the drama already. What did that woman want?"

"Shimon had a stroke. They admitted him to Soroka. He was unconscious for a couple of days. When he woke up, guess what the first thing he said to Kora was?"

"How should I know? It's too late for silly riddles. I just hope he's alright now."

"He's improving. The right side of his mouth is still slightly twisted. But don't worry, Kora will continue to love him with her undying devotion. He's fully conscious now, thank God. So, what do you think his first words were?"

"I don't know, you nag, what were they?"

"Waaater, *ya Fatma, jibu il mayim*, give me the water. Do you understand, *ya ochti*? After more than forty years." "I understand," I responded dryly, echoing him without further comment. His use of 'ya ochti', the Arabic term for 'my sister', hung in the air between us, a familiar endearment from our shared past. I hung up the call and sank into thought… When explained slowly, you grasp quickly enough, I mocked myself. After forty-some years...At

Long

Last

My

Penny

Dropped.

Was it real life or just fantasy

62

Lilach — Just Me and You

Lacrima's Secrets

My Childhood Days

A Dress for a Doll

Pnina Tel Dan

Lilach[5] – Just Me and You

"I don't understand what you want from me. I'm busy, caught between my grueling studies and Ayalet, who is a preemie, in case you forgot. She needs me all the time, you realize that, right? Then there's the house and Danny. I just don't have time to sit in cafés with you."

"But, Lilach, I just wanted to celebrate your birthday together, like we used to. I wanted us to have our own time. Quality time, just me and you," Paula said, her voice gargling in a desperate attempt to stifle her tears.

"I understand. But it just doesn't work out. Let's take a rain check. We're celebrating with the whole family on Saturday anyway."

"Lilach, listen. You're just being stubborn. I'll arrange everything. I got you a present. I'll come to 'Café-Café' in Haifa. It'll only be half an hour, tops. Ever since you got married, you've been drifting away from me. It's really

---

[5] In Hebrew, "Li" means "for me" and "Lach" means "for you." This linguistic nuance adds a playful element to the name "Lilach", which is a common name in Hebrew.

insulting... having to beg my daughter to spare half an hour for me."

"When will you get it? I'm your daughter, not your girlfriend. I need a mother, not a friend. I don't have time to go out during the week. I have my shift on Saturday, and I need to prepare the house, get everything ready. Why are you so insulted? Enough already, you're just being a nag. I'll see you on Saturday, bye…" Lilach hung up the phone, leaving Paula to stew in her indignation.

"Mom, Mom, you're so beautiful, and you're the best."

"Mom, I love you more than anything in the world."

"Mom, let's take the bus to Tel Aviv. Just me and you. We'll close up Tel Aviv and not let anyone else in. Not even Dad and Don. Just the two of us."

"Mom, look, I brought chocolate. For me and you. Come on, stop being so sad."

Paula wiped the tears that had silently streaked down her cheeks and soaked the slice of bread with jam that now sat orphaned on the plate resting on the glass kitchen table. She felt as if she had undergone a sort of earthquake. Clasping her hands in sorrow, she refused to accept the fact that her once special daughter was now replaced by a stranger, alienated from her. But who had replaced her?

How could she show such coolness? All I do is respond to her every whim, rushing to her aid like a soldier reporting for duty. Driving without a second thought from Jerusalem to Haifa, babysitting at only two or three hours' notice. Dropping everything to come running. And she can't make herself available for even a measly half hour?

Paula raised her eyes to her reflection in the glass pane of the kitchen cupboard — a white cupboard with a pine wood frame she had purchased about two months earlier from Regba Kitchens. Her alarmed expression, featureless and lacking distinction, seemed to share in her sorrow. Lilach regularly avoids speaking with me alone. Before she got married, she shared every little detail of her life with me and took an active interest in mine. We used to go shopping together, see movies, and she accompanied me to the theater. We used to spend hours talking in cafés.

Once, she said to me laughingly, "Mom, you're my living wallet." I ignored it, refusing to feel insulted. Just a poor joke of Lilach's. Or was it? In retrospect, this seemed like a warning sign, an omen for what was to come. Now here I am, truly feeling like a living wallet or an ATM. Feeling objectified, like a ragdoll tossed aside.

This ragdoll was still around but no longer the one and only. No longer that special doll, unique and significant in Lilach's world. She remembered to this day the stinging sense of insult she felt when Ayelet was born. Lilach demanded that she leave the delivery room. "I want to share this special moment with my husband alone. Understand, this is my firstborn daughter. It's an intimate moment. We want to be alone."

Despite the sharp pang in her chest, she kept her composure and exited, head bowed, to the waiting room. Before she left, near the delivery room hallway, she overheard the delivery nurse saying to the doctor, "That's the mother, I was sure she was the mother-in-law. Strange."

The sharp, foul smell of milk that had boiled over rushed her to the stove. The telephone conversation with Lilach before morning coffee surprised her, destroying her most precious moments of tranquility that preceded the storm, just before daily life would whirl her into its depth.

I have undoubtedly soured my relationship with Lilach. How could I have ignored all the early warning signs?

Now, looking back, she could identify a few, not necessarily in their order of occurrence:

"Mom, how long will you keep dyeing your hair?"

"You're such a drama queen, always needing to suck all the air out of the room."

"You always have to be the center of attention, don't you? Demanding constant focus. Sometimes I feel like I'm talking to Ayelet."

"Even before my wedding, you had to pull one of your 'Houdini' disappearing acts, being there without really being present for me, at your dysfunctional best. One would think a disaster had just happened, that someone had died and the family was preparing for a funeral and not a celebration. I asked Yael to help choose my wedding dress because I was embarrassed by your sour expression, and of course, you were offended. At least you cared, but apparently not enough to snap out of it and get a grip. And once again, you gave your best drama queen performance. Really, Mom, you were at your peak."

Such sentences uttered by Lilach appeared before her eyes as if written on an invisible screen each time she recalled them. She had seen something similar in one of the science fiction movies she used to watch with Lilach. These sentences burdened her with a heavy, melancholic distress.

That feeling of old age weighing down on her chest as she slept, becoming heavier with every passing minute, until she could barely breathe, waking up at the last moment, out of breath, slick with sweat, engulfed in a strange, undefined scent of fear and freezing cold. Even after waking, it took her a few moments to move her slowly thawing limbs.

After all these insulting sentences had steadied before her eyes, she felt that today the whirlwind of life would have to manage without her. Let it draw in someone else for a change. Today, she was pulling another one of her "Houdini acts." Today, she wanted to be dysfunctional rather than functional, and everyone — work, family, and especially Lilach — would just have to cope without her.

She wore the most worn and torn tracksuit she could find in the closet, grabbed a bar of nut chocolate, a cup of coffee, and left, laptop in hand, for the covered patio in the garden. And before sinking into her world, she remembered to call Mali to schedule an extra session on top of the regular weekly one, because now, more than ever, she needed Mali and the safe space she offered.

Was it real life or just fantasy

Pnina Tel Dan

Lacrima's Secrets

Slowly, she emerged from the house and hurried to the adjacent yard. It was Sunday. Julia had likely baked the chocolate cake with nuts and raisins that she loved so much. Each Sunday, in her parents' absence, she accepted Julia's invitation and slipped over to her house for their Sunday party.

Before the first slice of cake and a cup of cocoa, they would eat roast with potatoes and root vegetables accompanied by a quince compote. After the meal, if she agreed to eat the food served, they would go out to the spacious veranda and sit on the rocking chairs by the rectangular oak table. They ate with the relish and enjoyment of accomplices sharing a sinful, thick slice of chocolate cake with nuts, drinking hot cocoa made from real chocolate.

The summer sun caressed their skin as they listened to radio plays. Julia had tuned it in advance to a Sunday children's show in anticipation of Lacrima's visit. Just as story hour ended, Lacrima trembled with enjoyment tinged with sweet fear as she recalled the adventures of Red Riding Hood and the Big Bad Wolf. They chuckled, sang, and clapped their hands. They were delighted in each other's company during those stolen Sunday afternoon hours.

Julia leaned toward Lacrima, smiled at her, and said, "Wait here, Lacrimioare, I'm going inside to get your surprise."

A few minutes later, Julia returned holding a large rectangular box, wrapped in pink silk paper and tied with a gleaming white butterfly ribbon. Lacrima jumped up, eager and surprised, reaching out her hand to receive the large box. "Julia, it's not my birthday. Why did you buy me a present? It's so much fun being with you. You're really sweet. You're not at all like the witch that Mom says you..." Lacrima stopped mid-sentence, covering her mouth with her small hand. Her frightened eyes looked at Julia. She realized too late that she was about to reveal a secret her mother had forbidden her to disclose.

Julia smiled, pretended she hadn't heard, bent down to Lacrima, embraced her head, and kissed both her cheeks.

"Come, Lacrimioare, come open the box. Here, I'll help you untie the ribbon. There you go, now let's lift the lid together. Well, what do you say? Do you like it?"

Lacrima was stunned. Inside the box lay the most beautiful knitted dress she had ever seen. She widened her eyes and gazed at the dress, then at Julia. Words escaped her.

Julia looked at her and chuckled. She understood Lacrima's heart. The child was confused, barely understanding why she received such loving treatment from Julia, the very woman her mother regularly maligned. Lacrima's mother called her neighbor terrible names: Christian witch, Jew-hater, thief, and many others even worse.

Julia shared a wall and a yard with her neighbors and often heard Mrs. Dora, the neighbor, speaking ill of her and fabricating stories to tell Lacrima about her.

"That's right, sweet thing. This isn't your real birthday. You were born in March, in spring, during the joyful holiday of Purim, when everyone dresses up and give each other gifts of candy. But today marks the day I first saw you. A beautiful toddler with black, flowing curls, green slanted eyes, and a round face. You were about two years old. Suddenly, you appeared in my garden, asking to smell the flowers. To me, *you* were like a flower, just like the Lacrimioare, the lilies of the valley that I love to grow in my garden. I immediately gave you another name, Lacrimioare, a name your father loved very much and agreed to officially add to his and his wife's identity documents."

"So, this *is* a birthday gift, right, Julia? This is the day I was 'born' in your garden, only I was born two years old. What a pretty dress. Where did you buy it? I want to wear it..."

"My Lacrimioare, what do you mean, 'bought it'? I knitted it for you with my own hands. I have been knitting it for weeks. I chose this special pattern, echoing the flowers after which I named you. Come, raise your arms. We'll take off that old dress and put on your new one. Oh, sweetie, how pretty you look. How beautifully this dress suits you. If only my Lacrima could see you, she would surely have been very proud. Come, take a look at yourself in the mirror, my beauty..."

Lacrima followed Julia into the living room. On a wall by the window hung a huge, masterfully framed mirror. Its frame was greenish copper, adorned with flowers and birds suckling their nectar. Beside the mirror stood a dark boxwood chest, also engraved with various flowers and birds. White crochet napkins lay on the chest, atop which were placed photographs in silver frames.

Lacrima approached the large mirror and looked at herself. The dress was lovely and fitted her admirably. Proudly, she spun before the mirror to see how the dress swirled gracefully with her movements. She then went to Julia and hugged her legs. Julia lowered her head, and Lacrima gave her a kiss, full of gratitude for the gift and all the attention and love she had showered on her. Then she recalled Julia's earlier words.

"Julia, who is that other Lacrima you mentioned earlier? And why would she have been happy to see me in the dress you knitted for me?"

Julia bit her lip. Her mouth quivered, and tears streaked down her cheeks. She approached the chest, took one of the framed photographs from it, and showed it to the toddler.

Lacrima looked at the photograph and saw a very young woman with slanted eyes and black curls. The woman had a round face and distinctly red lips. She looked very familiar and seemed to smile at her warmly. Lacrima returned the smile.

"Julia, who is the woman in this picture? She looks so much like you, and her smile resembles yours. Why do you think she would have been proud to see me in this dress you knitted for me?"

Julia wiped her tears and gently placed the photograph back on the chest. After a few moments of silence, she petted Lacrima's head and said with a choked voice, "She is Lacrima too, my daughter. Or, she was... But let's talk about that another time. Now, you need to put back on your old dress and go home. I can hear your mother calling you. You can wear this new dress every time you visit me on Sundays."

Lacrima didn't argue. She knew she had to keep their Sunday parties and the special gift a secret from her mother.

This would be their secret, just hers and Julia's. Lacrima was experienced in keeping secrets. One more wouldn't be too burdensome. She hurried to sneak through the opening behind the strawberry and raspberry bushes back to her own home's garden.

Was it real life or just fantasy

Pnina Tel Dan

My Childhood Days

Julia's comforting embrace on the brown rocking chair, warmed by the wintery sun.

The spacious veranda. Our Sundays. The serenity, the birdsong, the verdant grass in the garden, the Lacrimioare flowers bowing their heads, barely containing their tears.

The scent of wood and the warmth from the scratched rocking chair; a very secret birthday just for me and my Julia.

A chocolate cake with nuts and a large, thick glass filled with steaming cocoa made from real chocolate, wafting its thick vapors that conjured up the bittersweet secrets of my childhood.

On a white macramé napkin atop the dresser, a woman is framed forever among silver embossed ornaments. Her slanted eyes, peeking through her black curls, are tender, their sadness incongruent with the smile on her red lips.

Six decades later, Lacrima is still with me, in the same silver frame, forever smiling.

For the first time, I notice the tears in her slanted eyes. I hadn't seen them back then, during our Sundays together.

Her pronounced lips forever keep the mystery of her life, hidden in the past's silver filigree.

My beautiful mother never had the opportunity to know me, yet even then she wept for her absence from mine and Julia's secret celebrations.

Pnina Tel Dan

A Dress for a Doll

Friday afternoon. The warm sunbeams heralding spring's arrival caressed the patrons of Piroska Café, its name evoking the Hungarian fairy tale character akin to Little Red Riding Hood. Liszt's bewitching melodies—Hungarian Rhapsody and Hungarian Fantasy — played in the background, imbuing the café with a European flair.

Crystal chandeliers dangled from the tall ceiling, adorned with plaster cornice curves, while landscape paintings by László Paál and his friend Munkácsy on the walls made guests feel as if they were in Budapest at the close of the previous century.

Scattered across the café were small, round wooden tables, carved and covered with tablecloths, accompanied by matching chairs. Each table held a white china vase adorned with macramé-like swirls, containing roses both white and red.

Friday afternoon. The sunbeams, heralding the celebration of spring just now beginning atop Mount Carmel, shone on the mount still drowsy from winter's grip — a winter that, a mere a few days before, had stubbornly refused to retreat.

By the café's wide window stood a small, round table, covered with a red-and-white plaid tablecloth. At the table sat a petite, roundish woman in her late fifties, her dark curls falling in disarray around her round face. Her slanted eyes held a dreamy expression, glowing in shades of green.

Friday afternoon, the trees of Mount Carmel glittered in the warm sun, their green foliage reflected in the woman's eyes. "What would you like to order, ma'am?" asked the waitress with a thick Hungarian accent. The woman's eyes twinkled, and she replied to the elderly waitress with bluish helmet-like hair in Hungarian, "Kérem szépen, van turós gombóc és szilvás gombóc" — cheese and plum dumplings, please. When the plate of warm dumplings was placed beside a glass of milk on her table, the woman inhaled their aroma with longing, savoring the sweet taste of bygone days, which melted in her mouth and flowed in rivulets of nostalgia through her veins, caressing the memories of her enchanting childhood onto her mature, slightly weary skin.

Her gaze fell upon a young couple trying to soothe their mischievous, black-curled daughter. A girl of about five, whose carefree laughter filled the café, evoking in the woman's eyes the playful spirit of another child — a little girl of similar age, from a lost time, a different afternoon, from a strange and otherworldly place, making the woman suddenly question whether it had ever really existed. Was it real life, or just a fantasy?

***

Sunday afternoon. Paula, a four-year-old girl, is seated in the middle of a lush green lawn. Surrounding her is a crown of tall trees with thick canopies in every shade of green. The colors of the tree foliage change with the angles of the falling sunbeams and the motion of the shadows, which crawl stealthily with the passage of time. Time itself moves serenely, almost coming to a standstill on this quiet island of happiness. The colors transition with spellbinding slowness — from the very bright, illuminated by the sun, to darker shades that are majestic and secretive, steeped in sweet reverence. The trees encircle her completely. The warm sun kisses her small, puffy cheeks. Lola sits beside her.

An onlooker might think they see two little four-year-old girls, close friends, seated in the middle of the lawn, sharing a marvelous secret. One girl, with black curls and a pale face, appears somewhat preoccupied. Lines of thought furrow her small forehead, while her tiny red lips, rose-like, form a circle expressing introspective wonder.

Suddenly, her expression changes, and a wide smile spreads across her round cheeks. Her slightly slanted eyes widen, and their greenish hue deepens. The sunbeams lend her a bewitched expression. At that moment, a spectacular idea sparks in her mind — something magnificent, explosive. A shocking magic trick that no one has ever performed before. A brilliant idea that fills her with endless joy.

Paula looks at her dress and caresses it. It's a deep indigo blue, velvety dress sprinkled with white circles the size of a medium coin. The dress has short, puffy sleeves that lend the girl an elegant, doll-like air. Prominent china-white buttons are sewn on the front, each adorned with an ornament of an ancient-looking anchor in blue and red. Paula adores her dress almost as much as she loves Lola.

Lola sits on the grass, embraced, her head resting on Paula's shoulder. Her stunning hair, a wheat-blonde mixed with reddish burnished brass, crowns her head like a wreath and falls in snakelike cascades around her perfect china face, down her shoulders, and along her back. Her face is beautiful. Her eyes, as blue as the sky and the sea combined, reflect the light into Paula's green eyes. Her red lips, picture-perfect, send a warm, mysterious smile to her friend. Unlike Paula, whose dress is lavish, Lola wears a plain white linen dress. This explains the troubled expression on Paula's face. Paula wishes, with every fiber of her being, for a twin sister who would look and dress just like her.

Together, they would create a unique world full of secrets — a beautiful, private island of pure joy, shrouded in mystery and grandeur. To this island, no one else would have access — they would seal it off, and no stranger would be allowed inside. The moment they both wore the same dress, exactly the same, they would not only be best friends but also true sisters, as similar as twins.

Filled with determination, Paula rose from the grass, pulling Lola with her. Together, resolutely and fully confident in their abilities, they headed to Paula's house to realize her enchanting vision.

It was a wonderful idea that no one but her had envisioned in the entire world. In their actions and uncompromising expressions, a sort of missionary zeal was apparent, bordering on the divine — a fervor akin to that of the children of Israel who stood obediently with Moses on the slopes of Mount Sinai. They accepted God's commandments without hesitation, proclaiming, 'We will do and we will hear.' Similarly, they devoted themselves to the idea with intense enthusiasm: all or nothing. It was the kind of absolute totality that only children can throw themselves into with such sacrificial fervor.

***

Upon entering the house, Paula placed Lola on the bed in her room. As Lola watched her actions with anxious anticipation, Paula hurried to her mother's room, grabbed the large scissors from the dresser, and quickly returned to her own room, slamming the door behind her. The window was open, allowing a warm breeze to flutter the transparent white curtain, inviting the sun and the treetops to peek curiously inside. A hush fell over the room. No birds chirped, no creatures stirred. The dolls, books, and all the other inhabitants of the room, including Lola, held their breath, intently following Paula's every move.

Paula decided to transform her beloved dress into two matching ones, one for her and one for Lola. With professional determination, she took up the scissors, and with fearless enthusiasm, she joyfully and resolutely cut her dress in half. The wind ruffled the window curtain again. Paula blinked; Lola looked on in horror. The magnificent vision, the magic of creation, dissipated with the breeze, vanishing in an instant. The two matching dresses, which the girls had glimpsed for a moment, disappeared. All that remained on the bed were two torn fragments of what was once Paula's beautiful, beloved dress.

Suddenly, the door burst open, and Paula's mother appeared in the doorway, holding a plate full of semolina dumplings stuffed with cheese and plums, topped with cream.

"There you are, sweetie… *Akarsz túrós gombócót vagy szilvás gombócót?* — would you like some cheese or plum dumplings?" she asked Paula. Upon seeing the torn remains of the dress on the bed, the plate slipped from her hands. The dumplings scattered across the carpet. She clasped her hands in astonishment, scarcely believing her eyes, and exclaimed in startled disbelief, "What have you done? Why did you cut the dress?"

"I performed a magic trick... I turned one dress into two, one for me and one for Lola. But the wind came and ruined the magic, leaving only these torn pieces. Right, Lola, weren't there two dresses just a moment ago?"

"How can one dress be turned into two of the same size without knowing how to cut and sew? Without a needle and thread? You've ruined your beautiful, only Sunday dress, for a doll? Girl, where is your head!? Why didn't you think before acting? Why didn't you ask? What will your *Apuka*, your daddy say?"

Her mother's tears mingled with those of Lola, who was deeply hurt by being referred to as just a doll. And Paula thought to herself, w*hat was there to think or ask? Everything was clear and understood; the magic had worked. It was only the wind's fault that it was lost.*

***

Years passed. Paula lay on her back in her spartan student dorm room in Beersheba, her hands resting on her belly, feeling Lilach stir within. Her belly was still flat. Just two weeks prior, she had received confirmation of what she had known for a full month — she was pregnant with Lilach.

Paula caressed her unborn daughter, who she had envisioned vividly in her mind's eye before she had even manifested in the reality of her womb. From the first weeks of her pregnancy, while reading Agnon's "Shira", Paula knew Lilach — her finest poem, her swan song — would be a delightful girl with curling, wheat-blonde hair tinged with reddish burnished brass. A strong child with eyes blue as the sky and sea; intelligent, inquisitive eyes, brimming with curiosity and boldness, always questioning.

On a nightmarish Tuesday morning at the start of her sixth month of pregnancy, as she finished climbing the stairs to the third floor of the Humanities Faculty to take an exam on Agnon's novels, she paused to catch her breath like Noah atop Mount Ararat. In front of a crowd that included her friends, her professor, and unsuspecting passersby, her waters broke in a mighty rush, flooding everyone in the stairwell below. Rattled and frightened, instead of heading to the hospital, Paula found herself at home, crying and curled up in a fetal position on her bed, seeking refuge.

As she waited for her partner Rubi amidst a nightmarish mirage of horrors, Paula felt the magic of Lilach's materialization beginning to fade, trickling away and vanishing abruptly. Consumed by a dreadful fear, she recalled the magic of the two wondrous dresses that had fluttered away in the wind, leaving behind only the tattered remains of her beloved dress on her childhood bed.

Less than half an hour later, Rubi, having heard about the flood at the Humanities building, stormed into the bedroom. Without wasting words, he carried Paula to a taxi waiting outside the dorms. At Soroka's emergency room, Dr. Lev, head of the maternity ward, declared decisively: "She's only in the sixth month of her pregnancy. The fetus won't survive. Prepare her immediately for an induced abortion."

What child is he talking about? What does he intend to do to my Lilach? Paula wondered in terror, a cold sweat covering her spine.

Dr. Shai Navon, Dr. Lev's intern, waited until the doctor moved on to disturb another innocent expectant mother's world, and then whispered to Paula with determination, "Don't listen to him. You can request to be kept on high-risk pregnancy watch here. Just sign a form releasing the hospital from liability. Spend a month or two in bed, take antibiotics, and you'll have your little doll to hold... Insist on it."

"But the doctor said otherwise," Paula replied, her voice choked with tears, her green eyes looking at the intern in total shock and despair.

"His wife," the intern pointed at Dr. Lev, "is also under high-risk supervision, in a situation similar to yours. He just wants to save the hospital money; it's all about the budget. Insist, and you'll see everything will turn out fine."

Paula wiped her tears, her shivering stopped, and a smile flickered across her eyes. With resolve and a sense of mission reminiscent of the zealous 'we will do and we will hear' biblical fervor from her childhood, she confronted Dr. Lev and demanded to sign the necessary forms to be admitted for high-risk pregnancy care.

***

After a month in high-risk maternity care, filled with engaging conversations and hatching future plans with her unborn Lilach, Paula went into labor, and Lilach was born at midnight on a Tuesday.

Days turned into weeks and months filled with turmoil. Paula watched her daughter through the incubator glass — a tiny, frail, hairy girl so emaciated that her bones protruded, bearing no resemblance to the beautiful child she had envisioned, fighting for her life. On one Tuesday, during her daily visit, Paula learned that her daughter was the strongest baby in the neonatal ward. However, due to a lack of space at Soroka's neonatal ward, Lilach was to be transferred to the Bikur Cholim Hospital in Jerusalem. Distraught, Paula, with Rubi's support, tried to overturn the decision but eventually had to accept it. She settled for weekly visits to the Bikur Cholim neonatal ward, where she closely followed Lilach's ongoing battle for survival.

Paula's weekly visits to Jerusalem were arduous. She watched her daughter lose weight, contract infections, and fight valiantly to cling to life. Each week, Paula left her home fraught with worry and returned to nights haunted by nightmares, where Lilach appeared, pleading for help, overwhelmed by her ailments. About two and a half months later, on another Tuesday, Paula found Lilach's incubator empty. Panicked and shaken, she feared the worst. As a silent scream threatened to burst from her chest, Nurse Ahuva entered, a joyful smile lighting up her face. In her arms, she held a plump baby, a beautiful blonde doll with deep blue eyes that mirrored the sky and sea. At last, her Lilach had truly materialized.

Cradling this perfect doll in her lap, Paula witnessed a miracle take form — a robust, vibrant child, fleshy and brimming with life, no longer fluttered and scattered by the whimsical winds of her enchanted childhood.

As time passed, her Lilach, her swan song, grew into a sweet little girl whose eyes reflected the sky and the depths of the sea. A curious child who, at every opportunity, proudly told anyone who would listen — and even those who wouldn't — that she was "studying in the university's kindergarten."

Was it real life or just fantasy

***

"Grandma, Grandma, here you are! We've been looking for you all over the café. Mom, I found her, I found Grandma Paula!" The woman by the round table was startled from her reverie and, with a wide smile and sparkling eyes, opened her arms to embrace her five-year-old granddaughter, a little girl with unruly golden curls and eyes the color of the sea and sky. "Lilach, why are you so late?" she asked her daughter, who stood next to her granddaughter, adding her own hug to the little one's. Then she leaned forward to her mother and planted a generous kiss on her cheek. "I've been waiting a long time. I even started on some of the cheese dumplings. We need to order more; these are cold."

The little curly-haired girl answered before her mother could, "Today, Mommy helped a woman with a baby in her belly who peed on the floor and cried. She gave her long pills, half-black and half-red, and promised her that in a month or two, she'll have a doll to hug, just like me."

"Lilach, can you explain what Ayelet is talking about? I swear, this child can spin some tales," Grandma laughed, raising her hands in mock despair.

"Ayelet is actually telling you about something that truly happened today. Just before my shift ended, after Yuval had dropped Ayelet at the hospital, we were by the entrance door when a young woman, about twenty, came in crying, claiming her water had broken and that the ER had sent her to us to schedule an induced abortion."

"Well, that brings back memories," the grandmother murmured, astonished.

86

"After examining her, I explained that with close monitoring in high-risk maternity care, she could still give birth, even if it might be premature," Lilach added, smiling as her chestnut hair joyfully danced on her shoulders. "To calm her down, after the initial treatment, we sat her in a wheelchair and took her on a tour of the preemie ward. She was amazed, looking at the premature babies developing in their incubators, yet still visibly worried."

"And then," Ayelet chimed in eagerly, "Mom told Naima that I was also born premature and lived for a few weeks in a glass house on wheels. It was warm and cozy there, and I grew up to be a normal baby. And I told Naima that Mom grew up just like me for a few weeks in the glass house and now she's a doctor. And when I grow up, I'm going to be a doctor just like Mom."

Grandma's eyes twinkled at her daughter's sea-and-sky-colored eyes. "As for being 'normal,' I'm not so sure…" she chuckled, picking up a shiny blue shopping bag from which silk wrapping paper peeked out.

"What's in the bag, Grandma?" Ayelet asked excitedly.

"A dress for my doll," Grandma laughed, pulling out her gift for her granddaughter. It was a small velvet dress in deep indigo blue, with short, puffy sleeves and white circles scattered across it. The dress featured a row of prominent white china buttons, each adorned with an antique-looking ornament.

Pini's Magical Garden

Miriam with a Heavy Moroccan Accent on the 'Mi', Pops a Balloon

A Group Photograph with a Curly Girl

Latifa

Pnina Tel Dan

Pini's Magical Garden

*"It is the mark of an educated mind to be able
to entertain a thought without accepting it."*
- attributed to Aristotle

Written as a tribute to all the pupils who have
survived, and especially to those who did not,
To the nurturing teachers who empower and
respect their students,
And as a whimsical reflection for all those
daunting teachers—
To all the Smart Alecks, wherever they may be.

Smart Aleck Comes to Fifth Grade

This was neither the first nor the last time my rebellious curls caused trouble. As I matured, though my curls lost some of their boldness due to the steamy humidity of a merciless summer day, my hair stubbornly reverted to its old ways. And perhaps this was due to *"Atlas Shrugged,"* which I eagerly read under the table during one particularly dreary literature lesson.

Here's how the story went: In eleventh grade, a new teacher arrived to teach our literature class — a retired officer, now a pensioner, who earned himself the nickname Smart Aleck (a fitting translation of the Hebrew "Tahkemoni Nevouvoni," mocking those who are all cleverness and no substance). He was in his late forties, a man of average height, with his bald head seamlessly extending into his neck. His shiny, yellowing scalp accentuated the yellow slits of his piercing eyes and his narrow-lipped mouth, which formed an isosceles triangle. His expression, along with the agility of his lithe body, perpetually glistening with sweat, gave him the air of a spineless creature crawling ominously through the corridors of our school.

Smart Aleck replaced Dr. Pinhas Navon, a beloved, nurturing, and supportive teacher who instilled knowledge and sparked interest. Dr. Navon's authority, emanating from his radiant personality, never interfered with his warm and respectful interactions with his students. After the previous principal retired, Dr. Navon became the head of our school.

From a literature class buzzing with engaging discussions, creative expressions, literary therapy, and creative writing, we were thrust into Smart Aleck's regime. He extinguished our love for literature. Instead of profound discussions, we were subjected to his fiery speeches that praised and exalted the necessity of committed literature, which must boldly and critically engage with societal issues.

Any author (or reader, for that matter) who engaged with poetic language, character development, or Ars Poetica was deemed a niche creator, whose work was considered marginal, trivial, and worthy only of scorn and derision.

Natan Zach[6] and the Anaconda Snake

In one literature lesson on an early June afternoon, the sun was impaled at the zenith, its beams flooding the classroom with the glaring remnants of the last poem slaughtered on the altar of teacher Smart Aleck's committed literature.

In the intellectual drought that pervaded our classroom, even the flies ended their lives with the elegance of a hedgehog on the dusty windows. Only Ayn Rand seemed to alleviate the despair.

Suddenly, I felt Zion Bar-Orian's elbow dig into my ribs. I looked up, and my desk mate pointed to a drawing in his literature notebook. It depicted a fearsome anaconda coiled around a poetry book by Natan Zach, its head uncannily resembling our teacher Smart Aleck. From its mouth, a speech bubble emerged: *"Social commentary is paramount. Literature that indulges in poetic frippery, capturing mere fragments of beauty, caters only to elite aesthetes who admire the beauty and virtuosity of words, with no substantial social message."*

Beside the drawing of the snake, I wrote the following:
Why did the math teacher's wife have to die?
I wish Smart Aleck would in her place lie,
Thus saving free thinking from being denied
While literature itself no longer had to hide,
And healing to our weary class provide.

We both burst into hysterical laughter until we heard the sharp hiss of Smart Aleck's words. "Shh… Silence in the classroom! Zion, would you care to share the joke with everyone?" Suddenly, his arm swooped down and snatched the notebook from our desk.

---

[6] Israeli poet. Widely regarded as one of the preeminent poets in the country's history.

Quiet fell. Smart Aleck turned pale, then flushed, rolled back his jacket, and slithered toward the blackboard, moving like a giant snake shedding its skin.[7]

"You two, stand up immediately, go to the library and write separate essays (and don't you dare copy from each other!) on the universal apologetics in Ronny Someck[8]'s poetry, focusing on the social divide. Each essay must be five printed pages and submitted by tomorrow morning."

Not knowing what came over me, I stood up, driven by some mischievous spirit, and declared, "I'll happily write the essay provided that Mr. Smart demonstrates his points and explains the interdisciplinary, existential, and apologetic message of the shaman in the book '*Journey to Ixtlan*'. And in general, I would greatly appreciate it if he could elaborate on this topic."

"Never in my life have I heard such a muddled mess of nonsense and such… rubbish," he snapped back, hissing.

"Perhaps you've never actually listened to your own literature classes, then…" I retorted with the daring of a kamikaze. The entire class shook with laughter, even the previously doomed flies seemed to resurrect.

"Out!" Mr. Smart shouted, "to Pini, C'est Fini!" (in Hebrew, he'd typically bark 'to kibinipini' — a nasty wordplay fusing 'kiton' for chamber with a vicious Russian curse). "You are expelled from this class for the rest of the year." Which meant one thing: go to Principal Dr. Pini Navon's chamber and await your punishment there.

---

[7] Inspired by Eli Eliyahu's poem '*Hameaklim*,' p. 13, from the book: Eliyahu, Eli. City and Fears. Am Oved, 2011, Tel Aviv."

[8] Israeli poet whose poetry often deals with social issues.

Pini's Magical Garden (Or, in Short: Pini, C'est Fini[9])

Dr. Navon's chamber was akin to an Aladdin's cave for literature lovers and those enchanted by its magic while waiting to be summoned for a meeting with him.

Students sent to Dr. Navon were expected to wait for hours on end in a small room heavily laden with books. Scattered on the tables, as if by chance, were books of various genres — belles-lettres, poetry, and non-fiction across diverse fields, including multiple branches of philosophy. Out of sheer boredom, pupils doomed to linger for hours might randomly pick a book from the table and start reading, often becoming engrossed in its captivating depths, forgetting the reason they were called to wait in the chamber and thus broadening their literary tastes and horizons.

Pini's chamber was a miraculous, enchanted garden where we delved into the wonders of literature and its charms under the delicate and insightful guidance of our beloved principal. He was an ever-present yet unobtrusive guide in our magical explorations.

After several hours, the door would softly open, and the principal's head would peek in. If he saw a student immersed in a book, he would gently close the door and only at the end of the school day allow them to go home. Not, however, before engaging in a conversation about the book's topic, discussing the student's literary views on it, and how, if at all, the book's theme related to their everyday life experiences. Often, the

---

[9] In French: It's over.

student would request to borrow the book for a few days to finish it.

At The Principal's Office

Still bursting with hysterical laughter, free from inhibitions and the cobwebs of didactic pedantry, we awaited our meeting with the principal. We were confident we had reached a safe haven, where we would typically spend a few magical hours with Carlos Castaneda and Don Juan on a Journey to Ixtlan.

However, at the end of the literature lesson, the secretary entered the chamber and led us to the principal's office. There, Mr. Smart awaited, sweating, his face pale and twisted with rage, red spots visible on his forehead and neck. After Mr. Smart recounted our misdemeanors during the lesson in our presence, Dr. Navon requested that we write a letter of apology to be published in the school newspaper. He also asked us to explain in the letter what had driven us to such disgraceful behavior. Additionally, we were suspended from literature classes for two whole weeks and required to make up the missed classwork independently. Instead of attending literature classes, we had to sit in the principal's waiting room until each lesson ended, lasting for the full two weeks.

Zion and I decided to write the letter of apology for the newspaper but also planned to publish the reasons for our behavior in the form of an interview with Mr. Smart, featuring a poetess of Mizrahi heritage — her Middle Eastern Jewish background standing in stark contrast to the dominant Ashkenazi European literary establishment. This would address some crucial literary topics.

The Letter of Apology and a Feuilleton

After two weeks of breathtaking and enlightening journeys in Pini's magical garden, the following apology was published in the school newspaper: *"We regret having vocally expressed our thoughts on Mr. Smart's teaching methods, and we doubly regret having written and illustrated our literature notebooks in a way that conveyed our opinions, our frustrations, and our feelings about Mr. Smart's personality and his impact on his students."* Additionally, we included a feuilleton that *"explains, though it does not justify, our disgraceful and exceedingly immature behavior."*

For those interested, I include here the feuilleton — that special section of light literary commentary and criticism — that was published alongside the letter of apology in the school newspaper:

An Interview with the Poetess Deborah the Prophetess[10]

Mr. Smart: Greetings, Debbie. I deeply appreciate you coming to our school to discuss your poetry. Like many others, I first encountered your work upon the publication of your recent book, *The Prophetess' Calling*.

Deborah the Prophetess: Sir, you do realize my name is not "Debbie," but "Deborah the Prophetess," correct?

Mr. Smart: Yes, yes, of course... Let's get back to the matter at hand. Initially, I believed that your poetry might represent a new and refreshing voice expressing the protest of the third and

---

[10] Deborah the Prophetess is a major figure in the Book of Judges, known as a wise leader, prophetess, and the only female judge of ancient Israel.

fourth generations of immigrants from Mizrahi countries. However, upon reading your poems, it became clear that they do not carry a social mission (as might mistakenly be expected from any artist of Mizrahi descent).

Deborah the Prophetess: Sir, are you aware that I am not a puppet pre-programmed to follow a script? Any mission my work might have is shaped by my personal life experiences, not dictated by seasoned critics of my poetry.

Mr. Smart: There's something about the tone and elegance in the imagery you use that carefully avoids being overly infused with Mizrahi elements. In my opinion, your unique voice deserves a respected place in Hebrew poetry. Many poems in your new book appear apologetic. I would like to ask: is this true? And if so, is this apologetic stance intentional? Furthermore, I would be grateful if you could expand a bit on this topic.

Deborah the Prophetess: I must confess that I don't fully grasp your point. Are you suggesting that grand themes such as fate, time, life and death, body and soul, memory, and parenthood — are reserved only for Ashkenazi poets, while Mizrahi poets are relegated to writing solely about their ethnicity or the vibrancy of their heritage?

Mr. Smart: Deborah, you misunderstand me. You have the potential to be a groundbreaking, whoresome poetess like Yona Wallach[11]. As both a woman and a Mizrahi, you could articulate, in an existential, apologetic, and interdisciplinary way, protest poetry about women's liberation, religious coercion, sexual

---

[11] Israeli poetess Yona Wallach was known for her revolutionary approach to language and form, challenging traditional norms in Hebrew poetry.

liberation, social divides, and the discrimination Mizrahi Jews face.

Deborah the Poetess: Sir, I assume you meant 'wholesome.' I wonder what Freud would say about your slip. Although I am a woman and a Mizrahi poetess, I am fully emancipated and thus do not need to carry this particular banner. Moreover, having been educated at the finest Western institutions, I do not feel the social rift or the oppressive weight of the Ashkenazi hand. Let me reiterate: I write from my own life experiences, and I'd be happy to expand on this during our discussion. Also, I'd appreciate it if you could avoid using professional jargon.

Mr. Smart: Why?

Deborah the Poetess: I graduated from high school last century, and it seems that now, in the modern era, the meanings of various terms have changed. I'm struggling to grasp your point. Both a woman and a Mizrahi... and also... because of the noise.

Mr. Smart: What noise?

Deborah the Poetess: The noise of *istra balagina kish kish karia.*

Mr. Smart: I don't speak Arabic.

Deborah the Poetess: It's Aramaic. The literal translation is 'a small coin in a big empty jar can make a lot of noise.'

Mr. Smart: How is that relevant? Deborah, spare me the proverbs. I'll tell you bluntly, without evasion: the social commentary in your poetry is weak, overly poetic, leans towards aesthetic indulgence, and is vague, although not devoid of beauty. It's literature for connoisseurs and elitists. True literature should carry a biting, bold message. The discerning, intelligent reader will opt for literature that champions social protest. This is literature at its finest — the only kind that will earn you respect and admiration.

Deborah the Poetess: I believe there's a place for a discussion about whether literature, like painting and sculpture, is inherently a form of art and thus justified in existing without being committed; or if it should indeed be committed to serve a political or social narrative. However, that is not why we are having this discussion. If you prefer committed literature, perhaps you should read literature influenced by Soviet communism or that served as propaganda for the Germans in WWII. I trust in the intelligence of readers to understand my poetry, hence I do not advocate 'biting' poems. And, as the saying goes, '*dai lehakima bermiza...*'

Mr. Smart: I've told you, I don't speak Arabic.

Deborah the Poetess: It's an Aramaic proverb, *dai lehakima bermiza (veleshatya bekurmiza)*. It means 'a hint is sufficient for the wise; a fool requires a punch.' I suspect even a punch wouldn't help in our case.

Mr. Smart: Listen, Deborah, I'm offering you the chance of a lifetime. Among my best friends are whoresome women, Mizrahi Jews, and dogs. Yona Wallach, who is also a friend, left a significant mark on modern Hebrew literature with her photo in tefillin with a man, transforming her into a daring and whoresome poetess. I can get you her tefillin and even a dog to make your photograph particularly striking and 'biting'. Add a *parochet*, a Torah ark curtain, with Mizrahi colors, and it will be a powerful social statement. Trust me, forget the proverbs and aesthetic niceties. A picture is worth a thousand words.

Deborah the Poetess: I have another proverb for you, this time in Hebrew.

Mr. Smart: Debbie, what proverb? Why another proverb? What does it have to do with our discussion? Forget the proverbs.

Deborah the Poetess: Silence is a fence around wisdom. Goodbye, sir.

Beside the feuilleton, we included a photo of an Oriental belly dancer wrapped in a Torah ark curtain. In a photomontage, we placed Mr. Smart's head on her body. Next to the dancer, we added a picture of Yona Wallach in leather clothes and tefillin — those ritual black leather prayer boxes worn traditionally by Jewish men — and also a particularly intimidating-looking dog with a fearsome, biting face.

At The Principal's Office Once More — Epilogue

Once again, we were summoned to the principal's office, this time to be sternly reprimanded. It was the first instance I heard the principal explicitly condemn our behavior. And yet, despite his harsh tone and stern expression, I could swear that behind the thick lenses of his glasses, deep within his blue eyes, there was a hint of bewilderment mixed with a faint, amused smile.

Mr. Smart demanded our immediate expulsion from the school. However, following a meeting that included our astonished parents, a compromise was reached. We were to be permanently expelled from all literature classes for the remainder of our high school years. Mr. Smart would not assist us with our final literature matriculation exams. Instead, we would prepare for the exams independently in Dr. Pini Navon's chamber and were required to submit essays on a variety of topics throughout the year.

The only instruction was to use terms and words we were familiar with and understood; otherwise, we would need to write an additional paper clarifying any term we misused.

Needless to say, we felt relieved and fortunate, and even though Mr. Smart intended to curse us, his curse turned into a blessing — echoing that ancient biblical moment when God turned Balaam's intended curses against Israel into words of blessing instead.

In time, at our graduation ceremony, alongside our diplomas in Literature and Philosophy, we also received awards for excellence. We received these honors along with Pini's warm embrace — he had accepted our invitation and attended the ceremony, extending his heartfelt wishes for our future success. We had also invited Mr. Smart, but guess who didn't show up?

Pnina Tel Dan

Miriam with a Heavy Moroccan Accent on the 'Mi', Pops a Balloon

How I Met Miriam

I met Miriam in a creative writing workshop during my MA in Literature at Tel Aviv University. The workshop was open to external students and attracted no few colorful characters. Miriam, distinct in both appearance and demeanor from other students, stood out even among the most extroverted. Since we both seemed to have landed there from another planet, we quickly became friends.

One day, while sitting together at the 'Horse in the Bar', Miriam shared her experiences starting her internship at a prestigious and well-known law firm. Here, I relay her story just as she narrated it to me.

Miriam Arrives to Work in the Big City

Yesterday, I began my internship at Kleinman and Weinroth, the hottest and most prestigious law firm in the country, known for handling white-collar crimes. A month ago, Professor Moshe Segal invited me to his office and mentioned he had recommended me to Weinroth as a top Dean's List student. The firm had accepted me as an intern, potentially leading to permanent employment — I felt like I had God by the balls.

I, Miriam Abukasis from the Katamon neighborhood in Jerusalem, the youngest daughter of Masouda and Yaish, immigrants from the city of Paz in Morocco, have come to the big city to work at one of the most sought-after firms in the country.

You know, Paula, my Grandma Sultana, may she rest in peace — kapara on her sweet, beautiful soul — used to say when I was just thirteen and had been admitted to Boyar High School, "You are the family's hot sauce, the only one from our neighborhood who's made it out. You will go far and bring honor to our family and people. Just remember, apple of my eye, don't become a thorn in their side, and never, ayouni, forget where you came from and the roots you carry. Be like still waters that run deep." Her words were peppered with affectionate terms like "kapara," an endearing Israeli slang originally used by Mizrahi Jews but now widespread, meaning something like "darling" or "sweetheart," and "ayouni," an Arabic term of endearment meaning "my eyes" or "my love."

The First Day – The Dream and Its Discontents

Yesterday, on my first day, I completed the second recruitment interview at Human Resources. I filled out forms and was briefed about the firm's ethos and my entitlements. Yael Weiner, the head of Human Resources, a stunning blonde with blue eyes, dressed in a sleek three-piece Prada suit, took me on a tour of the firm's four opulent floors. She introduced me to the staff as Miriam Abukasis, a promising Dean's List student from

Tel Aviv University, who would be interning under the supervision of Orit Kalman.

"Orit, this is Miriam, who prefers to go by Miri. She recently moved all the way from the Katamon Neighborhood to Givatayim. I'm entrusting her to your capable hands. I'm certain you'll polish this *sweet little thing*, this rough 'gem' as only you know how. And don't forget to bring her to the gallery after work," said the blonde, walking away without further ado.

I felt the stings of embarrassment spread through me, and my cheeks flushed red like the hraime sauce that Icho's mother heats on the Shabbat hot plate.

The impeccable blonde introduced me, with all the delicacy of a grater rubbing against an open wound, as the firm's new pet 'jewel in the rough' who had just arrived in the big city and whom "we must polish to conform to our standards and represent our values."

Her words, dripping with condescension, all but screamed 'Mizrahi' without actually uttering the term. The implication hung in the air, a palpable reminder of my Middle Eastern and North African Jewish heritage — a background she clearly viewed as something to be refined away rather than embraced.

Orit gave me a reassuring smile, gently pulling me out of my embarrassment, and explained that the firm's employees gather monthly at the P8 Gallery for a social event, where everyone could mingle over wine while enjoying cultural displays. "This time, in addition to the contemporary exhibits, we'll enjoy some of Klimt's works, including 'The Kiss,' 'Lady with a Fan,' 'Judith and the Head of Holofernes,' 'Judith II,' and 'Portrait of Adele Bloch-Bauer I.'"

Throughout the day, Orit briefed me on the files she managed, giving me a quick rundown of each client and our defense strategy. "Your role, Miri, is to help prepare these files for court, conduct research, find precedents that support our defense, secure necessary documents, liaise with client offices, and ultimately catalog everything into the firm's database."

Time sped by, and at six-thirty, after we had downed five cups of Turkish coffee *prepared by Orit,* we made our way to the luxurious restrooms to freshen up. After touching up our makeup, we strutted on our heels, sailing off to the gallery.

The Insult

Jerry Weinroth, one of the firm's two senior partners, a devastatingly charismatic figure, and a hottie to boot, kicked off the evening with a brief overview of the firm's recent accomplishments. He praised the "young and talented forces that have joined our firm" and wished everyone success in their work.

After the formal opening, I relaxed, mingling and introducing myself, enjoying the attention and background music. At the first chance, I slipped away with a glass of chilled white wine to admire the Klimt paintings.

As I moved past Klimt's portraits of women, I recalled what Eli, my art teacher at Boyar High School, had said: "Klimt has the sun in his belly." Only now did I truly understand his meaning.

Encapsulated in the fumes of white wine and Klimt's radiant heat, I headed back to the lobby. As I rounded the corner, I overheard Yael from Human Resources speaking to Idit, her secretary: "Have you seen that Miri? What an appearance! Black trousers and a white shirt, all those curls on her head, and the red string around her wrist - you know, that thing they wear for good luck and protection. Can you believe it?"

"She looks like a little waitress from some rundown development town. She probably never heard of a little black dress in her life. I just hope Orit will polish her up soon, or we're in for some real embarrassment."

"Next, she'll wrap herself in a flag, start clapping, and sing us the national anthem," Idit added her own dose of poison to the venom of Yeal, that plump two-faced ass-kisser from HR.

"You can take Miri out of the neighborhood, but you can't take the neighborhood out of Miri," Yael concluded with a smug laugh.

With tears in my eyes and icy fingers of dread twisting my guts, I rushed home to Icho, my compassionate femboy roommate, hoping her kindness and warmth might cleanse my soul of their scorn and the filth they had flung at me.

The Popping

The next morning, I arrived at the office in revealing jeans ripped at the knees and backside, a metallic belly shirt, hoop earrings, and my hair in a wild afro. Armed with nauseating pink Bazooka bubble gum for popping balloons and Zohar Argov[12]'s music on my flash drive.

My assigned room was directly opposite the offices of that two-faced, peaches-and-cream blonde Yael and her dim-witted secretary Idit.

I swung open the door, blasted Zohar Argov's music, and began typing into the computer.

---

[12] Zohar Argov was a renowned Israeli singer, celebrated for his distinctive voice and profound impact on the Mizrahi music genre.

It wasn't long before Idit stormed in. "Look, I don't think we've been introduced. I'm Idit — and please say my name with an accent on the last syllable. I'm the office manager for Yael Weiner. What's wrong with you, Miri? This isn't a nightclub. Stop that noise immediately. I am utterly appalled by you, absolutely shocked."

I spun around to face the ugly ass-kisser and popped a pink bubblegum balloon right in her face, the size of a watermelon. In my most pronounced Moroccan accent — stressing the first syllable of my name in a way that Ashkenazi Jews often mocked as showing poor education, despite it being a common trait among Jewish Moroccan immigrants — I retorted, "My name isn't Miri; it's Miriam. And now, before I start singing the national anthem and swat you like a fly from my room, remove that broomstick from your fat ass and fly out of here, you and your sugary sweet Weiner, straight out of my sight and back to your boiling witches' cauldron."

At Weinroth's

Not fifteen minutes had passed before I was summoned to Attorney Weinroth's office. Without unnecessary speeches or sanctimonious preachings, he demanded to know what had happened. Having already met me during my initial screening and being a close friend of Professor Segal, who had given warm recommendations on my behalf, Weinroth realized something was amiss.

With tears in my eyes, I told him about the patronizing way Yael had introduced me to everyone, and I also recounted, word for word, the corridor conversation I overheard from the two duplicitous bitches reigning over his human resources department.

"Look, Miriam with a heavy Moroccan accent on the 'Mi', our office has a dress and behavior code that we all must follow. Obviously, you're going home today and will return tomorrow as the exemplary Miri, the Dean's List intern I accepted into this office. You've made your point, but I wish you'd realized we didn't hire you because we need a token Mizrahi, but for your personality and skills.

"Despite their stunning little black dresses, Yael and Idit, though they both have law degrees, are mostly suited for office work. And despite all the nasty things they've said, they aren't truly evil bitches. They just vented their frustrations on you. In a few short years, you'll be living the dream that they'll never achieve.

"So, *yalla*, Miriam with an accent on the 'Mi', go home... my eyes are starting to get sore from that blazing lipstick and your metallic shirt. Tomorrow is a new day."

Feeling both shame and slight comfort, I quietly slipped out of Weinroth's office. I dodged through side corridors past the lawyers' offices, hoping Orit wouldn't see my pathetic 'Grease'-style Mizrahi bimbo disguise.

As I pedaled towards Givatayim, I felt the warmth of Klimt's sun and his 'Kiss' soothing my belly, dissipating the nausea from yesterday and the revulsion from my first encounter with the big city's cesspit vipers.

A Few Final Words for the Wise

I laughed with enjoyment hearing Miriam's story and found myself completely identifying with her. Now I understood why we clicked so instantly. We shared the same inclination to get into trouble with ourselves and the world. We both shared more than a few similarities in our extroverted behavior and our reactions to life's disappointments. Finally, we both navigated the urban swamp of Tel Aviv, often colliding headlong with the toads and toadettes thrashing within it.

Pnina Tel Dan

A Group Photograph with a Curly Girl

I look at the black-and-white photo. On an elevated platform, children stand in three rows — boys and girls about seven years old — at their mid-year first-grade party. They are all dressed in the folkloric attire of rural dancers.

The year is 1964. I gaze at the group of children. Among them, one short-statured girl stands out, her head crowned with black curls. Even the still photo, freezing time through the camera's lens, fails to contain the bounce of her curls. I close my eyes, remembering... Her face is very pale, tension evident on her tightly stretched skin across her cheekbones. Her hands are balled into fists at her sides, her eyes bright green, sparkling with determination, a slight wrinkle visible above the bridge of her nose, and her lips pursed.

Through closed eyes, I sense the clean scent of snow. The clean twilight light reflects the whiteness of the snow, still gleaming and striking my senses with its freshness. Tall, bare trees have long forgotten their golden crowns, their tops now barren with the passing of autumn. The bright light fades, merging with the crisp, clean, and cold scent.

The reddening beauty of the sky stirs in my soul the splendor the girl in the photograph witnessed on her way from her home, accompanied by her mother, father, and brother. They all hurried to the first-grade talent show.

The girl remembers the route well, for it has been a month since she was assigned her role in the school play. Every morning, her mother walks with her to school, taking the longer path, to help her memorize her lines. The curly-haired girl grew resentful, angry, and rebellious: she always gets the least desirable roles. Among the shortest in her class, if not the shortest, she is both Jewish and Hungarian, the only one among classmates who despise Jews and Hungarians. She is always placed at the back in every show or performance. The best roles — princesses, queens, and fairies — are always given to the taller Romanian girls.

"As if it wasn't enough that they are the tallest, they always stand in the front row. And me? I've had to recite this silly speech about a diligent ant and a dumb grasshopper every morning for a month. Mom, enough... it's not important... it doesn't even fit the story in the play. I know it by heart now, and besides, no one will see or hear me because I'm at the back."

"You must perform whatever role you are given to the best of your ability. You need to know your part as well as you can. You're no longer a little girl doing nonsense and silly things like you did on Mario's birthday."

Suddenly, peals of laughter burst from within me. I direct my gaze into the eyes of the curly girl looking at me from the photo, and I see her on a sunny spring Sunday, in the warm noon of her older brother's eighth birthday party, who is three years her senior.

Guests and family members sit on the veranda around a round dining table made of dark mahogany. The veranda overlooks a lush garden adorned with white bellflowers, red poppies, and tall, dark green, damp grass gleaming in the sunlight. The scent of roasted meat on the table mingles with the aroma of a chocolate cake baking in the oven's heat. These smells fill my nostrils, conjuring forgotten memories.

To my utter astonishment, the five-year-old curly girl pushes aside her brother, who is reciting a poem by Romanian poet Eminescu, climbs onto a chair, and without the slightest confusion, in a completely confident and professional gibberish, recites in front of the guests, claiming the spotlight for herself. Amid bursts of laughter and the crowd's cheers, she steps down from the chair and gracefully performs a lively Csárdás Hungarian dance as her encore.

I shake my head and look again at the photograph, hearing through the veil of time the calm voice of the mother, endlessly patient: "Enough, you are now a big girl, you need to know your role, you can't act like a funny little girl anymore." I gaze back at the photograph, wondering what happened to all those little Romanians and all the blond girls who so effortlessly became the princesses and fairies of their childhoods. I admit I'm somewhat puzzled, how is the curly girl photographed at the front of the stage, in the front row?

I close my eyes, trying to make sense of the visions I conjure in the darkness. Suddenly, the children's clothes in the photograph turn red, green, and golden blue. Their bodies are covered with white silk shirts embroidered with a plethora of colors, their hair adorned with white ribbons tied in butterfly knots, the scent of new, clean clothes and shiny leather shoes filling the air. The hall is packed with the children's parents and siblings. The principal speaks, congratulating the young actors and the esteemed teacher for their contributions to the performance.

In the background, Leopold Mozart's Toy Symphony plays. The red velvet curtain slowly rises, and the fairy, the princess, and the prince proudly recite their lines. Suddenly, a small, short girl with defiant curls pushes her way from the third row to the front of the stage, her fists clenched, and with fierce anger, begins to recite part of the princess's role... Noise, commotion, laughter bursts from the audience. Her mother is shocked. Her father and brother burst into laughter, but the curly girl, undeterred, firmly claims her place at the forefront of the stage.

I open my eyes, wondering how the audacious girl wasn't afraid of the inevitable punishment from her teacher and her mother. I remember that with her immigration to Israel in 1965, the curly girl continued to fight for her right to be seen and heard.

Over the years, as she approached adolescence, the girl lost her bouncy, rebellious curls. With the loss of her curls, her boldness and determination also seemed to fade.

As she grew up and faced life's upheavals, the girl-woman accepted the restrictive reins of a limiting reality. Right and wrong became clearer, and with them, the recognition that not everything is possible or permissible.

Her somewhat wavy hair faintly reminded her of the boundary-breaking, liberating antics of the curly girl, whom she often missed with an uncompromising, illogical longing.

Sometimes, in her dreams, the woman with wavy hair stretches out her arms longingly and embraces the daring curly girl, whose curls fearlessly broke the conventions of the permissible and the forbidden.

I open my eyes and look again at the photograph, smiling at the little audacious girl. I could swear that the little rebel smiles back at me, winking mischievously, reminding me of the enlightenment I experienced long ago.

Though my hair is wavy and lacking curls, I've found within me again those bouncy, rebellious curls. Curls full of life, allowing me to be bold, to try new things, to say goodbye to weary events, to choose originality, creativity, to let curiosity bubble within me like fine champagne, in anticipation of new and challenging endeavors.

And if I need to claim the front of the stage to be heard and to influence, to be seen and to be noticed, I do not hesitate to do so.

I reconnect with the uncompromising daring of that girl with the unstoppable spring in her curls. "I love you, my little curly girl, and I hope that you will never, ever disappear on me again."

Was it real life or just fantasy

Pnina Tel Dan

Latifa

I have to admit, I really lost it today. I decided to put everything down in writing because I just had to vent. I tried to understand how I could have behaved in such a shameful way, haunted by paranoia and fear of strangers, fearing everything that's different. It all began in the early afternoon.

I went with Liran to pick up Tzlil from kindergarten. She fell asleep on the way back, the sweet thing. When we got home, just as I laid Liran down in her bed, a long, persistent ring invaded our home. Tzlil was playing with his Legos in his room. I hurried to the door, hoping Liran wouldn't wake up, yet I didn't forget to take the usual safety precautions.

I peeped through the peephole. A stranger stood behind the door. Although it was a warm and sunny winter day, the narrow corridor made it difficult to make out the feminine figure staring back at me through the peephole. I noticed a broad, toothy smile, and heard a nearly childish voice, with an Arabic accent, pressing through the locked door: "Madam... *ya sit*, please *biddi maye, iftah il bab, min fadlak.*" The words, a mix of Arabic and broken English, floated through the air — "I want water, open

115

the door, please" — a desperate plea in a language not quite her own.

"Maya? I don't know any Maya," I said hurriedly, distraught by my two and a half months old daughter Liran's cries, which relentlessly tore at my frayed nerves and squeezed my headache into the only brain cell I had left after childbirth.

She had cried nonstop for half an hour all the way to Tzlil's kindergarten. On the way back, she finally fell asleep. I hoped that after the Tylenol I gave her to reduce her fever, she would take her afternoon nap. Then I could finally get around to tidying up the house and working on my seminar paper — "Representation of the Foreign and Alienation in Hebrew Literature" — which was just sitting there molding on my laptop.

A pealing laughter cut through my thoughts, rolling into my small, cluttered student apartment. "*La, la, la, ana ismi Latifa. Ana eatshan,*" she chirped in Arabic, meaning "No, no, no, my name is Latifa. I'm thirsty," before switching back to English, "please, a drink...

"With frantic gestures, I asked five-year-old Tzlil to stay in his room and whispered to him: "Sweetie, go check that Liran hasn't woken up."

I took a quick glance at my small apartment, seeing it was in no state to receive guests. On the blue shaggy carpet in the living room, a pile of books and children's toys were scattered. On the couches and rattan sofa, piles of children's clothes and reusable diapers I had just taken out of the dryer lay strewn. No, there was no way I was letting some Arab stranger, whose language and intentions I couldn't understand, into my personal hellish chaos.

Yet, she did sound like a helpless young woman, I thought to myself, and decided, perhaps too rashly, to respond to her humane request. "Just a minute, I'll get you a bottle of water," I shouted, rushing to fetch a half-empty water bottle from the fridge, while the chaos in the kitchen cruelly assailed me again. The baby formula and unwashed baby bottles on the kitchen table, the counter overwhelmed with groceries I hadn't yet managed to store.

I cracked the door open, forgetting, as usual, the safety chain, and offered the water bottle to the young woman standing before me.

Ignoring my extended hand, she wedged her foot in the door and, before I could react, pushed past me and burst into my home. She danced around the room, whirling and breaking into a rhythmic Arabic song. "*Wald hilou, tifl hilou, Latifa hilwe,*" she sang to me with a beguiling smile, the Arabic words meaning "Sweet child, sweet baby, Latifa is beautiful." She fervently repeated the mantra: "*Beit helou, inti Jamila, wald hilou, Latifa hilwe, tifl hilou,*" her song proclaiming "Sweet house, you are beautiful, sweet child, beautiful Latifa, beautiful baby" in her native tongue.

Though I was thoroughly terrified, I realized something was very wrong with the young woman who had barged into my house. Before me stood a teen, about eighteen, tall and slender, dressed in a black velvet Bedouin jellabiya embroidered around the neck and chest with colorful flowers. Her beautiful, dark face was framed by long, black curly hair. Her lips were a deep scarlet, well-defined and prominent, and three thin green lines were tattooed on her chin.

As the sound of the stranger's singing filled the room, Tzlil came out of Liran's room and gazed at the young woman with bewildered eyes. She continued to sing, muttering various incantations in Arabic and dancing around the carpet.

"Mom, who is this girl? She's going to wake Liran up," he said in an anxious tone, a mix of astonishment and fear in his voice. "Ask her to be quiet," he added, pressing against my leg. The intruder ignored us and kept dancing. Every so often, she flashed an innocent smile and burst into rolling laughter. Whenever her eyes landed on a toy she fancied, she bent down, picked it up with an exclamation of delight, pressed it to her chest, and rocked it as if it were a baby, all while continuing her dance around the room.

Despite my pity for her, I realized things were spiraling out of control. Even though I tried to gently direct Latifa toward the still-open door to leave the apartment, she gracefully evaded my grasp and continued her frenzied cavorting around us. Her large eyes, rimmed with black, shadowed by dense, long lashes, continued to smile, and her unbridled laughter echoed through our small apartment, threatening to wake Liran.

"Latifa, you're going to wake the baby. You really need to go now," I raised my voice at her, but she continued to ignore me.

Suddenly, Liran's cries came from the next room. Before I could rush to protect her, Latifa sprinted like a woman possessed into the children's room, leaned over Liran's crib, and began to rock it while singing her mantra: "*Tifl hilou, Latifa hilou, Latifa bahebak, tifl hilou...*" Her Arabic lullaby, a gentle stream of "Sweet baby, Sweet Latifa, Latifa loved sweet baby," filled the air, its meaning as soothing as its melody.

Panic overtook me, and I felt I was losing control. I feared I might lash out at her any moment; I couldn't predict the behavior of this unexpected, uninvited guest. Filled with a maddened rage, like a lioness sensing a threat to her cubs, I tried desperately to get her away from my children. My nerves, frayed from the lack of sleep since Liran's birth two and a half months ago and weighed down by household and academic responsibilities, signaled clear and immediate danger to my children. I had to protect them from the madness that had invaded our home.

Losing all control, bursting with anxiety, I screamed at Latifa, "Don't touch her, do you hear me? *Latifa, rouh min beit!*" The Arabic command to leave this house burst from my lips, surprising even myself with its intensity.

As my uncontrollable cries echoed throughout the building, I heard hurried footsteps coming up the stairwell. To my immense relief and embarrassment, I saw Orna, our neighbor from the apartment across ours. Orna, a close friend and a resident in community medicine at Soroka Hospital, entered my apartment, gave me a reassuring look, and murmured as she passed by, "Calm down, Amira, I've got this."

She went straight to my messy kitchen, grabbed the fresh baguette lying on the table, tore off half, spread some butter found in the fridge on it, sprinkled a little salt, and handed it to Latifa with a calming smile.

The young woman finally stood up from Liran's crib, holding Regina the Ragdoll in one arm and the baguette in her other hand. With a grateful smile, she said, "*Shukran, Sit* Orna," her Arabic words of thanks and respect softly punctuating the tense atmosphere.

As she rocked the doll like it was a baby, she finally stopped dancing, collapsed to the floor in the corner of the room, and began to eat the bread.

With Tzlil, both terrified and mesmerized, clinging firmly to my leg, I quickly picked up the weeping Liran from her cradle and sat down with a sigh of relief in the rocking chair.

"Bread with butter or any other spread is the only thing that calms her when she's in such a state," Orna clarified.

"Where do you know her from? How did she get here? Why did the guard at the student dormitories' door let her in? Is she dangerous?" I bombarded Orna with softly whispered questions, as I did not wish to rouse the 'Sufi whirling devil' from its slumber. The phrase brought to mind those mystical Islamic dancers who spin in meditative rituals, seeking a direct connection with God — a fitting metaphor for the unpredictable force we feared awakening.

"Latifa was born in Tel Sheva to the Ator tribe. She has been diagnosed with severe mental and emotional challenges. Aisha, Latifa's mother, assists Bruria, our housemother, with cleaning maintenance in the D section of the student dormitories. I have already called Bruria, and Aisha is on her way here to pick up her daughter."

"Madam Orna, Madam *hilwe*, please, *biddi maye*," Latifa smiled at us, her voice calm, her body leaning over the rag doll showing care and love for the baby she held to her bosom. Her Arabic words, meaning "beautiful Madam, please give me water," flowed gently. Orna returned from the living room with a water bottle and handed it to Latifa. Latifa set down the baguette and, without taking her gaze from the baby even for a moment, drank deeply from the bottle, handed it back to Orna, and politely added, "*Shukran, shukran,*" her repeated thanks in Arabic hanging in the air. Then she resumed eating while continuously rocking and kissing Regina the Rag Doll.

As we watched, speechless, Latifa's surreal behavior as she showered her baby with love, Aisha stormed up the stairs and, still breathless, entered the room. Aisha, a tall, impressive woman radiating strength, wrapped in a black jellabiya, her head and shoulders covered by a white hijab and a look of concern on her face, turned to Orna and me and said, "Sorry, sorry, my *binti* is not quite right, Allah has stroked Latifa's head," the woman explained, her words carrying a playful double meaning in Hebrew where 'litef' means 'stroked', cleverly alluding to Latifa's name and condition. "She runs from me all the time. Madam Sit Orna, please explain to Sit Sasson. My Hebrew not very good."

"Latifa was born mentally challenged," Orna explained, "and at sixteen, her father married her off to her fifty-year-old uncle as his second wife. The uncle began abusing her on the very first night, and he has been beating her ever since. Her mother, to protect her, brings Latifa with her to work and gives half her salary to the uncle."

"Her *baba*," Aisha added angrily, "married her to brother, and I did not want."

"Now, as if all this wasn't enough," Orna continued, "Latifa is also pregnant, and her mental state has worsened because they changed her medication."

"Is she dangerous?" I asked Orna.

"No, I don't think she's dangerous, but she needs constant supervision, being mentally challenged and functioning like a five-year-old. I provide therapy to the family as part of my internship as a community doctor in Tel Sheva," Orna continued her story while gently stroking Latifa's curls.

Aisha turned to her daughter and resolutely got her on her feet, showering her with words of endearment mixed with soft chiding. From her body language, and following Orna's explanations, I understood that Aisha was urging her daughter to return the rag doll and apologize. Latifa raised her eyes to me, showing all the world's sorrows, reluctantly handed me the rag doll, and murmured, "*Samah li*, madam," her Arabic plea for forgiveness barely audible. She then added, "*Shukran, hilwe* madam, *shukran*, Orna, *shukran ktir-ktir*," her words a cascade of gratitude in Arabic, thanking the "beautiful madam" and Orna "very-very much."

I smiled at Latifa, stroked her cheek, and handed back the rag doll. A smile broke out on her face, and she left the apartment with joyous cheers and spirited Sufi dancing.

And we, we remained stunned and shaken, as if a hurricane had whirled over us, leaving us on a shore, wrung out and emptied of strength, swamped with mixed feelings of relief, estrangement, and gnawing sadness…

Was it real life or just fantasy

Pnina Tel Dan

The Purple Room

*Inspired by the stories of Edgar Allan Poe, with a particular
nod to his short story, "Berenice."*

In the autumn of 1999, I traveled to the resort town of Klagenfurt
in southern Austria. The plane landed at the local airport at
23:00. The airport was deserted, except for the mustached driver
wearing a brown suit, a flat cap of the same color carelessly
resting on his short, black, parted curls. He waited for me in the
deserted arrivals hall, holding a sign with my name on it.

He introduced himself as Eddie and smiled thinly behind his
mustache. The smile did not reach his intense black eyes. He
looked familiar, but I could not place where I had seen him
before. Eddie patiently waited with me by the baggage claim,
and about a half-hour later, he collected my luggage from the
carousel and led me to a long, black limousine. He opened the
back door for me and helped me get settled comfortably. *Phew...
what style*, I thought to myself, amused.

The organizers of the conference I was invited to certainly
did not spare any expense. The conference was organized to
commemorate the legacy and works of Edgar Allan Poe,
marking one hundred and fifty years since his death. We drove
straight to the WortherSee Schlosshotel, which had been
reserved for me by the conference organizers.

As we drove all the way there in almost complete darkness, I saw none of the landscapes that, according to Herr Karl Schultz, the chairman of the association, were among the most breathtakingly picturesque in all of Austria. We arrived at the hotel after midnight, and despite the darkness, I could make out, thanks to the street lamps illuminating the vast courtyard, that it was a large, ancient castle hotel with turrets rising above it and baroque-style decorations adorning its façade.

The castle was enclosed by a fortified wall, inside which giant trees with monstrously thick trunks and dense foliage grew. Eddie carried my suitcases inside and rang the desk bell. The place seemed deserted and shadowy. A few minutes later, the receptionist appeared, his eyes dimmed with fatigue. He yawned an apology, turned on the lights in the lobby, asked for my passport, barely glanced at it, and quickly completed the registration process.

"Madam Anabel Belee, we have reserved the Lilac Suite for you. It also includes an adjoining study."

"Anat Belau," I corrected him quickly, with an amused smile.

"I hope everything is to your satisfaction."

"Thank you," I muttered tiredly and hurried after my luggage bearer to my room.

I showered, put on the dark purple velvet robe, and slipped into the matching slippers laid at the edge of the massive canopy bed in the middle of the bedroom.

The suite, styled in an ancient, somewhat Gothic fashion, boasted a tall ceiling adorned with plaster and wood cornices at its corners. After the refreshing shower, I felt completely rejuvenated. I poured myself a bit of champagne, sampled the fruit plate on the low coffee table, and wandered around the large suite.

The suite's layout included a huge bedroom, a spacious living room, a study, a dining area, and a bathroom equipped with a jacuzzi, a steam room, and a luxurious shower, complete with all the sophisticated 'toys' designed to pamper the hotel's distinguished guests. The separate toilets were designed in an ancient Gothic style, with brass taps shaped like swan heads showing signs of corrosion. To complete the antique look, all the sanitary fittings were styled in an archaic 19th-century fashion.

I was amazed by the entire suite's palette of purples: aquarelle pale purple, lavender, and a deep velvety purple that almost touched on regal burgundy. The suite was lavishly carpeted with soft, deep rugs. Velvet purple sofas, benches, and lounge chairs were scattered throughout the space. Mahogany cabinets and closets carved with geometric patterns of arabesques, leaves, and roses completed the somber ambiance. In niches within the walls — clad in silky, brocade lavender wallpaper — stood candlesticks, their bases sculpted into figures of devils and idols from Etruscan and Egyptian mythology. These candlesticks cast a soft, yellowish light that dimmed the space further. The table lamps, crafted from wood and marble, featured motifs of the goddess Astarte and of wolves and cats, predominantly in black. Paintings in carved, gilded frames adorned the walls, depicting canonical scenes from the New Testament: Adam, Eve, and the serpent in the Garden of Eden before the expulsion, the Madonna and child, among other scenes I did not recognize.

I had never encountered such a ghastly and cluttered array of items in any other hotel. "They've certainly gone overboard with this heavy Baroque-Gothic style," I remarked to my reflection, which peered back at me amusingly from the mirror beside the study, naturally styled in the same manner.

Despite the late hour, I felt invigorated and decided to review the lecture I was to deliver the next day at two o'clock in the Berenice conference hall at Klagenfurt University. The lecture's theme was "Gothic Elements in the Stories of Edgar Allan Poe."

With a glass of champagne in one hand and my laptop in the other, I entered the study, an oval-shaped room dominated by shades of dark purple. Against the wall, in front of the heavy, dark desk adorned with carved wooden animal heads, hung a portrait of Edgar Allan Poe. Flanking his portrait were paintings of a man on one side and a woman on the other. The woman was tall and extremely slender, her face narrow and hollow, her complexion pale and smooth. Her eyes were completely expressionless, her very high forehead crowned with thick, curly yellow hair that draped over her gray dress. Her gaunt lips, lifeless, stretched into a chilling smile, revealing thirty-two long, narrow teeth dazzlingly white. The man's facial features in the adjacent painting bore a slight resemblance to those of the woman. He was lean and tall, dressed in a white shirt and a black frock coat, his dark black hair curly and parted on the right side of his head. His broad, high forehead shone palely, and beneath his black mustache, his narrow, red lips protruded. His black eyes, shining with an unexplained madness, pierced me, casting an uncomfortable sensation.

I then realized the man's portrait resembled Edgar Allan Poe, and both paintings vaguely reminded me of someone I had seemingly met recently. Despite my efforts, I couldn't remember who it was.

This room, too, featured table lamps with bases shaped like wolves or black cats. Red masks bearing animal features and Etruscan vases of various sizes, decorated in azure and turquoise, were scattered throughout. As I sat down and opened my laptop, the yellow lights in the room began to flicker on and off, intensifying my unease.

I must have dozed off for a few moments. When I looked around the room again, I noticed the gilded frames of the paintings were empty. I found myself seated on one of the chairs, bound by wide purple velvet straps. Above me, a rhythmic, inexplicable noise whirled. I looked up to see a swinging pendulum, its end shaped like a sharp guillotine blade slowly descending towards my head. Cold sweat streamed down my spine as I trembled in terror, listening to the furious, screaming voice repeatedly shouting, "What a bunch of nonsense, Professor Belee." "Belau," I corrected weakly, lifting my gaze anxiously.

Right before my eyes, Edgar Allan Poe materialized, flanked by the man and the woman from the paintings. Waving my lecture notes furiously, he repetitively barked, "A muddle of nonsense! A decadent rot of odious thoughts. Tell me, please, is this what they teach in the Comparative Literature Department at Tel Aviv University? Is this what you plan to present in your lecture tomorrow about my life's work?"

The man in the portrait glared at me with his fiercely raging eyes and nodded in agreement with Poe's literary critique. The woman also looked at me with her expressionless eyes, her horrifying smile widening as she bared her white teeth menacingly.

"Why don't you understand, being such a 'distinguished Professor,' that at the core of all my stories, beyond the Gothic elements, lies madness, the obsessive compulsive impulses of the protagonists, their necrophilic tendencies toward female characters? I insist that you mention in your lecture that I am the preeminent author of horror stories. I am the writer of death!" he screamed manically, his spit flying towards me, his eyes emitting terror, and his curls wildly flapping around his face. "I suggest you quote Ibn Zaiat's Latin epigraph from my short story 'Berenice': *'Dicebant mihi sodales si sepulchrum amicae visitarem, curas meas aliquantulum fore levatas'*—'My companions told me that visiting the grave of my friend might somewhat alleviate my sorrows.' If not..." Poe didn't finish his sentence, but the menacing look he gave to the pendulum made his intentions clear.

Throughout this bizarre lecture of terror, the pendulum ominously kept descending towards me.

"Excuse me, Mr. Poe," I addressed him with a faint, trembling voice, as despite my dreadful situation, my intellectual curiosity urged me to ask, "How exactly will adding this epigraph to my lecture clarify your point about the compulsive nature of your protagonists and your title as the ultimate writer of death?"

Both figures from the paintings hissed in disdain and moved threateningly closer, the pendulum steadily nearing my neck. Suddenly, the lights began flickering again. A terrifying ring shattered the tense atmosphere in the room.

I snapped awake, still trembling with fear and drenched in sweat. Confused, I lifted my head and saw that I was in the purple room, the figures securely in their gilded frames, with no sign of the pendulum or the eerie ambiance.

Through the white, transparent curtains, the first rays of an autumn morning gently caressed the room. It seemed I had fallen asleep. I needed to get ready for my lecture. *What a nightmarish dream,* I smiled to myself in relief. My thoughts were interrupted by a ring at the door. I got up, stretched, walked to the suite's entrance, and peered through the peephole. I caught sight of a stranger behind the door. On a second look, noticed the tall, thin chambermaid in gray uniforms. I recognized her only when she pursed her thin lips into that dreadful smile, revealing thirty-two long, narrow, brilliantly white teeth.

Was it real life or just fantasy

Pnina Tel Dan

Raphael

I crossed the verdant green lawn, sheltered by weeping willows that draped over the space like a mourner's tent, enveloping the wide, whitewashed house. It was a pear-shaped structure — its form echoing the Hebrew word 'Agasi' which is also a surname — with a red-tiled roof and shutters painted a Mediterranean blue. Those shutters brought to mind the fishermen's houses on the beaches of Agia Kyriaki in the Greek Pelion Peninsula. This picturesque village, nestled beside an endlessly white sandy shore, was where Raphael and I spent our last vacation together before our military draft.

Hesitantly, I ascended the house stairs. At the heavy oak door, I paused, debating whether to use the black cast iron knocker or ring the bell. Part of me wanted to turn back and run, but I had no choice — I had to enter. Standing before the Agasi family's door, I noticed a blue-eyed Hamsa on the frame, the palm-shaped amulet popular throughout the Middle East and North Africa that symbolizes protection and is traditionally believed to ward off the evil eye. Although it had disappointed, the household's good luck charm still hung there defiantly, a symbol of hope unfulfilled.

The Agasi household was my second home, where I experienced the happiest days of my life alongside Raphael, my best friend who was more like a brother. His family had adopted me, enveloping me with warmth and love. For someone introverted like me, the only child of Holocaust survivor parents from Poland, such warmth was not to be taken for granted.

It had been five years since I last visited, and I hadn't even made a phone call. After our vacation in Greece, both of us had enlisted: I joined the Intelligence Corps, and Raphael, insisting on combat, joined the Golani Brigade. During an operation, his armored personnel carrier hit a landmine. Raphael, the sole survivor, was confined to a wheelchair for life. After his release from the Beit Loewenstein rehabilitation center, I spent most of my vacations with him in his family home. However, our meetings became increasingly strained. Raphael often secluded himself in his room and spoke little. About five years ago, during one of my final visits, he requested that I stop coming.

"You see," he explained, "you remind me of who I was and what I could have been. The laughter, the good times, the sunshine, and the pretty girls on the beach. The future that will never be mine. It's too much. I love you like a brother, Nahche, but I can't start to resent you. So please, just stop coming."

I honored his request and abruptly cut ties not only with him but also with his family, as he had wished. Honestly, I felt a mixed sense of relief and guilt, relieved to have escaped a situation that had become unbearable for me.

Now, I was compelled to enter and face them; I had no other choice. Sweat spread up my shirt from under my armpits, the stench engulfing me. It reminded me of a corpse, or someone condemned, aware that their final moments were imminent, their body prematurely releasing its secretions out of weakness or fear. The label on my T-shirt began to itch; I scratched my neck frantically, the unbearable irritation intensifying.

Taking a deep breath, I pressed down on the door handle, entered decisively, and made my way to the subdued voices in the living room, hurriedly sitting down on the only available chair.

The room was filled with both familiar and unfamiliar faces, young and old, gathered in a circle on low black chairs labeled 'Yad Sarah' — an Israeli nonprofit organization known for providing free or low-cost medical equipment and support services to those in need.

Initially, I could hardly register any details or make sense of the conversations, which sounded muffled as if through a seashell. After a few minutes, I recognized Raphael's family — Jinet, Eli, and Tuli (Tehila), his sister — on the low, cushionless sofa. They were pulling photographs from a beautifully crafted wooden box, the box of memories that Raphael and I shared, examining the images and passing them around to the condoling visitors.

One of the photos reached my hands, and I saw Raphael, an impressive man: tall, dark, athletically built, with striking, handsome features and hazelnut brown eyes. Black curls framed his face. His lips, sensuous beyond the chiseled lines of his features, were spread in a wide, vibrant smile.

Beside him stood Diana, true to her namesake, the Greek goddess of the hunt — tall, slender, with black hair cascading past her waist. Raphael's left arm embraced my shoulders, those of a young, slender youth with straight, fair hair and slightly slanted, dark eyes. My own face bore the same carefree smile, one arm around my brother's shoulder, the other holding Donna, the voluptuous redhead from Scotland who had joined our circle.

Together, the four musketeers, we had spent about a month on the beach, frolicking in the blue waves, hopping from bar to café, and exploring the intimacies of our bodies between the sheets in Greece that pre-military summer.

A hard lump rose from my stomach to my throat, and tears clouded my eyes.

Suddenly, I felt a comforting hand on my shoulder, and Tuli's voice as she spoke to her parents, "I knew he'd come for the shiva. There was no way he'd hear about Raphael and not show up."

As I looked up, Tuli pulled me closer. Before I could respond, I was enveloped by the arms of my second family. I had expected anger, or at least some coldness for my abrupt departure, but instead, they surrounded me with the warmth I had sorely missed. Jinet, noticing my discomfort, gently stroked my forehead and explained that Raphael had left a letter detailing why had had asked me to cut all ties and move on. "I think Raphael was right, although it was hard to understand at first — now it all makes sense. He wanted to bow out at his peak and didn't want you entangled, fearing it would affect your life's path. He loved you dearly, as we all do. We're all you have left. There's no need for you to keep your distance. Right, Tuli? Nahche is always welcome here, and in your home too, isn't he? Did you know Tuli got married last year and she's expecting in four months?"

My heart pounded; I couldn't speak, only hug them all and mumble congratulations to Tuli, a gesture that, under the circumstances, only highlighted my awkwardness and our collective Kafkaesque predicament.

"How did you find out about Raphael?" Tuli asked, her eyes, mirroring Raphael's hazelnut gaze, fixed on me. Sweet Tuli had blossomed from a charming girl into a stunningly beautiful young woman, as captivating as her brother. Through her Raphael eyes, she perpetuated my loss, a loss we all shared.

"We were on vacation in London, and when I opened the Haaretz newspaper on my iPad, I saw the article about his death. I'm sorry I couldn't make it to the funeral…"

"Don't be sorry; at least you were spared the whole ordeal with the Chevra Kadisha," Jinet sighed. "The Jewish burial society responsible for preparing the deceased wanted to bury him outside the cemetery fence. It's an old tradition reflecting the community's disapproval of suicide, based on the belief that life is sacred. We finally laid him to rest in the 'Right Rest' secular cemetery, near Kfar Saba."

Eli reached into the wooden box and, before I could caution him, pulled out a blue velvet bag, tugging at its silk ribbon.

"What's this, Nahche?" he asked curiously.

A burst of frenetic laughter echoed among the mourners. It was the laugh bag we'd bought on the island and used to embarrass people in the bars we loved. Eli blanched as the laughter sliced through the room like a whip, making me lose my contact with reality again. The others shifted uncomfortably in their chairs. Then Tuli burst out laughing. "It's just like Raphael to have the last laugh," she said, throwing the laugh bag through the open window onto the lawn. Everyone laughed again and sighed in relief. The tension that had built up moments earlier dissipated.

"Come, Menachem, Sufika has made us couscous. Let's eat before the Mincha prayer," Eli said. "During Shiva, they hold this daily afternoon service here at home to accommodate us mourners."

As the four of us sat around the kitchen table, Tuli revealed that a few months after I stopped visiting, Raphael's depression had intensified, and he had needed medication. "He must have planned everything in advance. It appears he hoarded pills, and during one of his crises, he swallowed them. The next morning, when Dad brought him tea in bed, he couldn't wake him up."

Tuli suddenly produced a white envelope from the pocket of her long skirt and handed it to Menachem. "He left you a letter, as I was sure you'd come to the shiva..."

At the end of the meal, after I read Raphael's letter aloud, we all wept with gnawing pain, and grief descended on us like a black pashmina scarf, suffocating us with our inconsolable loss. At Eli's request, I joined the minyan, the quorum of ten Jewish men required for prayer services, that gathered to pray Minha in Raphael's room. Eli handed me Raphael's yarmulke, the skullcap worn for religious reasons, and his tallit, the prayer shawl used during prayers. His comforting hand rested on my shoulder. Together, we prayed from Raphael's prayer book. In the midst of the prayer, a loud peal of church bells pierced the murmured recitations of the worshippers. I froze for a moment, catching the angry glares of the other men directed at me. My sweaty palms struggled to pull my iPhone from the back pocket of my pants.

"Sorry, sorry," I muttered, "it must be my youngest; I forgot to turn off my phone, I am really sorry," I continued, as a strange, metallic scent wafted from my mouth with each word. My mouth suddenly dried, and the foul smell mixed urgently with my apologies in the crowded, agitated space.

Finally, I managed to extract my iPhone, but in my embarrassment, instead of hitting the red button to reject the call,

I accidentally pressed the green one and the speakerphone at the same time.

A child's voice emerged from the device. "Dad, where are you? You promised to finish telling me the story about the lion who loved strawberries…"

"I can't, Raphael, I'm in the middle of a prayer. Sorry, sweetheart, we'll continue the story tomorrow," I whispered hurriedly, and finally silenced the dreadful device.

Sweating, with the odd metallic taste lingering in my mouth, uncertain where to hide my shame or how to escape the accusing, judgmental stares of the worshippers, I suddenly found myself enveloped in Eli's embrace, wrapped together in Raphael's tallit.

"Menachem, you named your son after our Raphael. May you be blessed, may the Lord comfort you and increase your descendants. May you never know sorrow again," the grieving father consoled me softly, his tear-filled eyes —Raphael's hazelnut eyes — looking at me with accepting reconciliation.

Was it real life or just fantasy

Raphael's Letter

Dear Nahche, our friendship is wonderful, surpassing even the love of women[13]. If our sweet Tuli has passed this letter to you, then you have managed to get to my Shiva and despite the difficulty, despite our loss — yours, mine and actually all of ours — I believe, or want to believe, that you have found comfort. That you have all found each other again. Be strong and love each other intensely, unconditionally.

I hope that you are finally in peace originating from acceptance. This letter, dear Menachem, is a sort of operation manual, a sort of will that you must read and sanctify. But before that, I owe you an explanation. And also… please, be the one who explains to my family the reasoning behind my actions.

I well know that it has been unbearably difficult for you to respect my final request to sever ties with me and with my family. But I felt that alongside the difficulty was also a certain relief. The encounters with me became unbearable for you and for me… for both of us.

---

[13] This alludes to the biblical account of David and Jonathan, where the phrase 'surpassing even the love of women' highlights the deep and profound friendship between the two.

Please understand, if our situation were reversed, I would feel exactly the same as you do (we've always said we shared a hivemind, haha). I have no resentment toward you for having agreed to accept my demand without fighting for me.

I could not share my true situation with you. Even my family members did not know, and do not know still, anything about my health. You all assumed (and I allowed you to maintain these assumptions) that I am depressed for being wheelchair-bound; for not being the same dashing womanizer, the life of the party, the heartbreaker, the strong optimistic man with a promising future. This was all true, but only partially. If this were the only difficulty, I would have reconciled with it, overcome it, tried to squeeze some honey from the comb that fate provided me. But the truth was much grimmer.

After recovering from my injury and transferred to rehabilitation, my condition worsened without any reasonable explanation from the doctors. After routine tests that yielded no answers, it was decided to carry out a painful procedure called a lumbar puncture.

The results of these tests and a blood test yielded antibodies for autoimmune diseases. I will not linger on the medical terms. Both conditions had nestled in my body since birth, and the trauma caused by my severe injury triggered their outbreak. Apparently, these had spread in my brain causing severe cognitive issues, worsening my depression. My eyesight rapidly deteriorated, and cancerous growths were discovered in my pancreas and liver.

The doctors predicted that I would become a severely ill, bedridden patient, blind and paralyzed, suffering excruciating pains due to the deadly cancer that had already metastasized.

They claimed I would need to be hospitalized in a few months in a geriatric hospital.

I knew that both you and my family would commit yourselves to treating me, a severely ill patient, at the family home. I was unwilling to live a prolonged life of suffering, without a shred of humanity, devoid of hope, becoming a heavy burden on you and ruining the lives of those I love most.

Please forgive me for having taken responsibility and cutting short my life before the upturning sword of Damocles would ruin all your lives. The future that awaited me and all of you was unbearable, and thus, I felt my choice, though perhaps controversial, was the only solution.

And now, Nahche, I command you, or rather plead with you, this: if you have not yet done so, please continue to live. Live on. Fulfill yourself. Live for both of us.

Realize your destiny. Fall in love. Love for both of us, start a family, and if fate, or the god or goddess of fertility would gift you with a son, please give him my name.

Be a son to my family, and let your son be the comfort they need as if he were their own grandson.

This way, I will know that I have a descendant to continue my legacy through you.

One last request: forgive me again for my harsh behavior during our last meetings. I did it intentionally to push you away. Now, during the Shiva, act as my spokesperson and explain to my family what I have clarified for you in this letter-manual-will.

Be like a son to them, let them enjoy you and your family, so that your infectious laughter may once again fill the Agasi home. Let them join you without regret, able to love again, reconciled with the past, comforted, and hopeful for the future that awaits.

And I hope — here I am sentimental and unexpectedly cliché — that somehow, I will continue to watch over you, enjoying your happiness and keeping you safe from any harm or misfortune.

Farewell, my brother, my beloved, your love is more wonderful than that which Jonathan had for David. Farewell, my dear beloved family, stay safe until that blessed day comes, when we will meet again, each in his or her time, after a long, healthy, happy life lived to the fullest.

Forever your brother, Raphael.

Lola, Death Awaits You at the End of the Street

In the midst of a midsummer Sunday, little curly-haired Lacrima[14] ambled around her house's yard, bored to the bone. She had already thrown stones at Fritzie, the neighbor's mewling cat; sneaked into the kitchen to devour the semolina cookies reserved for guests; licked a spoonful of salt; and exchanged secrets with Lola. Yet, she was still bored to death. What she hadn't yet done, and was decidedly planning to, was to tease Julia.

Julia, her Romanian neighbor, was an elderly woman in her late fifties. Having spent most of her life in Timişoara, a large university city in Romania, she remained, and would always remain, a nosy, coarse, Jew-hating woman.

---

[14] Lacrima, or Lacrimiora, means 'tear' in Romanian, named after the flower 'Tears of Our Lady.' This refers to the tears of the Virgin Mary weeping over the suffering of her son, Jesus, who atones for the sins of humanity. The stalky flower, which lowers its head, has rows of small, white flowers that resemble tears dripping down to quench the earth's thirst. The secular Jews of Romania, having been educated in Christian establishments, are thus familiar with Christian lore.

145

"It's so boring," Lacrima complained to Lola (or Lolita, as her mother called her). "Mom's not home, Dad's out visiting friends, Mario is over at Ryan's as usual, and it's just you and I left hanging out here alone. You know what, Lola? Let's go to Mihai Bácsi.[15]"

Lola looked at her incredulously, silently reminding Lacrima of her mother's stern warning against leaving the yard alone to venture out into the street.

"Don't be such a drag. Come on, let's go visit Uncle Mihai, you know who I mean, the uncle who lives at the end of the street. You know him. He always sits on a low bench by the gate of his house. Uncle Mihai has the most fascinating stories, and toffees, caramel, and milk chocolates. He also has a sweet dog, Chuchu, who can wag, stand on his hind legs, and roll over. It'll be fun, so come on, let's go."

Sweet Lola silently acquiesced to Lacrima's suggestion. They peeked inside the house to make sure Maria, the plump and lazy housekeeper who had recently arrived from a neighboring village, was still passionately kissing Igor, the dark-haired, brawny milkman.

Stealthily, the two crossed the yard, their little feet pattering over the moist grass strewn with bellflowers in vibrant colors and Lacrimioare, "the tears of our lady," flowers lamenting humanity's sins. They moved through Julia's yard and onto the path leading to the end of the street, towards Uncle Mihai.

The sun, high at the zenith, shocked by the irresponsible behavior of the two little mischief-makers, cast its sternest beams of warning at them, reminding them of Lacrima's mother's strict prohibition on leaving the yard — and most

---

[15] In Hungarian: Uncle Mihai.

certainly forbidding them, had she known, from approaching Uncle Mihai. He sat at the street's end, weaving his seductive webs, waiting to ensnare the innocent neighborhood children.

Lacrima whispered again with Lola, and together they decided that before they would visit Uncle Mihai to sample his suspiciously generously offered toffee and caramel sweets, they should first stop by their neighbor Julia's garden to pick some of her tempting fruit for the road.

Turning on their heels, they headed back to the rear part of the house their family shared with Julia, and cautiously snuck into Julia's garden through the back gate. They passed by the succulent raspberry bushes, indulged in the red raspberries, and didn't spare the black ones either. Then, they headed towards the strawberry bushes—the pride of Julia's garden, the apple of her eye.

The rich juice stained their chins in shades of red, black, and velvety burgundy, redecorating their snow-white dresses, which had been gleaming with cleanliness just moments before. Now, it seemed as though someone had splattered their blood, spreading it across their faces, down their necks, and onto their dresses, arms, and hands — as if they had just stepped out of a nightmarish horror movie.

Suddenly, they heard the raspy voice of Julia as she emerged from the colonnaded porch, striding briskly toward them while wielding a menacing witch's broom above her head, as if it were the Sword of Damocles threatening to behead the two impudent little girls.

Lola and Lacrima glanced at Julia, then at each other, and burst into peals of loud laughter and joyful cries, "Come on, Lola, let's run. The witch has mounted her broom and is coming to chase us. Let's get away quickly!"

The two naughty girls sprinted from the garden like arrows, while Julia — in her black, torn, and tattered house dress that had seen better days, and with her hooked nose featuring a large, black, hairy mole — chased after them, flailing her arms. Her rageful swings of the broom and bursts of curses could have shamed the loudest peddler in any marketplace.

As Julia watched heartbreakingly the torn remnants of her strawberry and raspberry bushes, the little bandits sailed on with peals of laughter and cheerful cries, leaving their neighbor to bitterly mourn the loss of the bushes she had stolen from Lacrima's family last winter and planted in her own garden.

All her plans for making raspberry and strawberry jam for the cold winter days now dripped from the cute chins of the mischievous thieves. In their hurried escape, Lacrima turned and squealed with delight, "It's not stealing if it's already stolen!"

Still bursting with laughter, soured by the red-black blood of the bushes they had summarily executed minutes earlier, they joyfully approached Uncle Mihai.

Uncle Mihai, sitting on his low bench, resembled a Humpty Dumpty who, tired of his repeated falls from the wall, had decided to give up and nap in the sun.

At the sound of the two pranksters, both stained and dripping with thick, sticky juice, Uncle Mihai opened his eyes. He gazed in bewilderment at their faces, flushed from eating the forbidden fruit, which seemed to thrill them immensely. The two little sprites looked like an accident waiting to happen.

A smile spread across Mihai's puffy face, which had the yellow texture of an aging wax candle, revealing poorly kept teeth whose bad odor followed him wherever he went.

"Would you like some candy? I have new types of toffees: fruity, chocolate, and bubblegum. Come, sweeties, come sit with

Uncle Mihai. Uncle Mihai will tell you interesting stories, then we'll go inside, eat chocolates, and play games. Would you like that?"

Lola suddenly turned serious, a cloud of concern shadowing her beautiful china face. She tried to signal warnings to Lacrima, but Lacrima was too caught up and excited to notice.

With determination, Lacrima pulled Lola and followed Uncle Mihai, who laboriously rose from his stool and lumbered towards his house.

Uncle Mihai opened the heavy wooden door, which creaked as it swung. From inside the dim house wafted an unappealing smell of mold, lack of air, and dirt. The two little pranksters wrinkled their sweet noses in disgust.

Curiosity filled Lacrima, as it was her first time entering Uncle Mihai's house. She anticipated discovering enormous piles of various flavored toffees, chocolates, games, and especially Chuchu, Uncle Mihai's adorable dog.

On the table, which hadn't been cleared since breakfast, rested three plates with old toffees and a bar of dark chocolate. There was no sign of Chuchu or the games Uncle Mihai had promised.

"Where's Chuchu?" Lacrima asked, her voice choked with tears. "Where are the games? Why aren't you opening your windows? It's dark in here and it smells bad."

"Auntie Mina took Chuchu to the doctor. He wasn't feeling well after eating all the new toffees and chocolate I bought yesterday. But we don't need Chuchu. We can play a different game," he suggested. His tone took on a disturbing quality as he began to recite:

"Let's play a game that's oh so fun,
Where gentle touches have begun.
 Beneath your clothes, a secret zone,
A special game for us alone."
The sinister implications hung in the air.

"It's too dark here for Lola, and she wants to go home, so we're leaving," Lacrima stated firmly, pulling Lola behind her.

"Lola is tired, and she wants to rest," Uncle Mihai said, separating Lola from Lacrima and placing her on the sofa beside him. He extended his hands, sat Lacrima on his knees, and tickled her down her back under her dress.

"Well, doesn't it feel pleasant? Doesn't it feel nice? After the game, you will get a beautiful present from Uncle Mihai. Isn't it nice to play at 'down the hand goes to make you feel good under your clothes?'"

The truth was, if not for the disgusting smell of the dark, musty house, and if not for the revulsion she felt from the yellowish, wax-like touch of Mihai Bácsi, and the stench of his rotting teeth, she might have even enjoyed his warm attention and the pleasant sensation down her back.

His tickle-caress subtly triggered near-pleasant currents along the nerves of her exposed, defenseless body.

Yet, when she glanced at Lola, who lay on the sofa next to Uncle Mihai, a shadow passed over Lacrima's pale face, and her black curls bounced in discomfort.

Lola's eyes, deep as the sky and sea, signaled to Lacrima, "Come on, we're going home... Mom said we mustn't let other people touch our bodies. We need to run back home. Double quick."

"Uncle Mihai," Lacrima said, "I hear Daddy calling Lola and me from the yard. We need to go home or we'll be punished. Come on, Lola, we're leaving."

Lacrima pulled down her dress, slid off Uncle Mihai's knees, grabbed Lola's hand, and helped her off the sofa. Without saying goodbye, she pushed the old, heavy wooden door open, dashed to the yard dragging the shocked Lola behind her. Slamming the rusty iron gate shut without looking back — for fear that Uncle Mihai's furious gaze might turn her into a pillar of salt — she ran until she reached her warm, safe room, breathless and terrified.

There, in her cozy bed, she curled up in a fetal position, thumb in mouth, and while clutching Lola to her trembling body, fell asleep from sheer exhaustion. Her face was still marked with the juice of forbidden fruits, and tears unwittingly traced paths of guilt and nameless fear down her cheeks.

About two hours later, Lacrima opened her eyes. Through the open window of her room, she saw the green foliage swaying in the evening breeze and the rustling of leaves. The sun had descended from its zenith. The world was still bathed in light, but it was no longer the harsh midday sun; it was a gentler, more forgiving light.

Lacrima rubbed her eyes and lifted Lola, who had rolled off in her sleep and fallen onto the carpet.

"Mommy must have come back from her shift at the Securitate[16]. It's annoying that even on a Sunday, when everyone else is off, Mommy has to leave us to be bored by ourselves at home. Right, Lola? Let's go tell her what happened at Uncle Mihai's."

---

[16] Securitate: Romanian secret service.

Lacrima took Lola's hand, and together they stepped out onto the large front veranda. Their mother was setting the table — plates, glasses, cutlery — for the Sunday afternoon meal. The round wooden table was covered with a bright, white tablecloth. Hearing the patter of their little feet, she turned, saw Lacrima and Lola, and a cry escaped her lips as she rushed to lift them both into her arms.

"What happened, Lacrimioara? Did you fall? Were you hurt? Where have you been? Maria has been looking for you since noon."

"We were there..." Lacrima pointed toward Uncle Mihai, who, as usual, was sitting on his low stool leaning against his yard gate. His gaze was fixed on the mother and daughter, whose voices carried to him from the end of the street.

"Lola and I visited Uncle Mihai this afternoon," Lacrima explained. Her mother's face clouded over, she removed Lola from Lacrima's side, and sat her on the veranda railing. With a look of deep concern, she drew closer to her daughter and asked in disbelief, "What? Where have you been? Didn't I tell you never to leave our yard? What were you doing at Uncle Mihai's? I explicitly told you not to go there alone. What happened to you, child? Where is all this blood from? Did someone hit you?"

"No, no one hit me. It's just from Julia's raspberries and strawberries. Lola and I tasted some before we went to Uncle Mihai's."

Her mother clasped her hands, her expression a mix of worry and anger, nearly choking on her words, "You pestered Julia again and stole her fruit? Am I going to have another argument with the neighbor who shares our wall and yard? Haven't your father and I told you countless times not to go into her garden, not to touch her strawberry and raspberry bushes? Now I'll have to bake a cake and apologize to her again. When will you grow up? How many times must I tell you? This time you will face the consequences — you won't be allowed to play with Lola for a whole week."

The tearful Lacrima quickly approached Lola, who sat on the balcony rail, trying to mitigate the harsh punishment as she knew she couldn't bear a week apart from her beloved Lola. She raised her hand and pointed angrily at Uncle Mihai, shouting, "You're upset about this, but you ignore the fact that you leave us alone and that Uncle Mihai played 'Let's play a game that's oh so fun, where gentle touches have begun…' with us? That's nothing to you, right?... You said no one should touch our bodies, and he, an adult, did! But you say nothing to him and only punish me and Lola for a few stupid strawberries and raspberries that Julia stole from our yard last year... And stealing from a thief isn't really stealing. This is all Uncle Mihai's fault. And you don't punish Uncle Mihai because you borrow money for milk from him when you run out at the end of the month. I wish, I truly wish he'd die and be buried in Hitler's grave," Lacrima cried out in fury, pointing again toward Uncle Mihai, who strained his ears from his house trying to catch the details of their argument.

The gusts of furious wind grew stronger, buffeting Lacrima's accusing hand and inadvertently striking Lola too. Suddenly, a harsh blow was heard. Lola fell from the veranda rail and hit the curbstone at the edge of the lawn, three meters below.

Shocked, Lacrima and her mother rushed down, and to their horror, found Lola's perfectly beautiful china face and her lovely sky and sea eyes shattered at the foot of the veranda.

"Lola's dead, Lola's dead!" screamed Lacrima, trembling all over as an uncontrollable flood of tears streamed down her face.

Her mother embraced her, reassuring that Lola wasn't dead, just injured. She promised to take Lola to Uncle Nicolai's clinic and that within a week she would return home healthy and whole.

On Tuesday morning, the week Lola was hospitalized at Uncle Nicolai's clinic, Lacrima and her mother were on their way to kindergarten. As they passed by Uncle Mihai's wicket at the street's end, the rusty gate opened, and out came Aunt Mina — a woman in her early sixties, her hair disheveled, eyes red and teary, her nose running — as she clasped her hands in grief.

"Mrs. Kalman, Mrs. Kalman, a terrible disaster has happened. I woke up this morning, and my poor Mihai… Please come in and see for yourself," she pleaded.

Lacrima's mother followed Aunt Mina inside, still holding her daughter's hand, who clung to her dress in deep fear. They entered a hall where the smell of mold mixed with the suffocating scent of wax from lit candles scattered around a sofa in the room's center overwhelmed mother and daughter.

On that sofa, where Lacrima had sat on Uncle Mihai's knees just days before, lay Uncle Mihai on his back, looking like an upturned whale with a massively swollen belly, dressed in a black suit, his face bloated, eyes closed, his skin as yellow as the wax candles burning around him. He appeared to be sleeping, his open mouth forming a large drool balloon.

"When did he pass away?" asked her mother.

"I woke up this morning, tried to wake him with a cup of hot coffee like I do every day, but he didn't respond. I called Dr. Ionescu, who came and declared him dead on the spot. Dr.

Ionescu said he died of a stroke overnight, which was to be expected given his excessive weight — the result of many nights of gorging himself with food and drink and his unhealthy lifestyle," Aunt Mina explained.

Lacrima, trembling uncontrollably, barely registered Aunt Mina's words. She only remembered that because of Uncle Mihai's actions, Lola was now so badly injured, lying in Uncle Nicolai's clinic. She also recalled her own curses, wishing him dead in Hitler's grave. Distressed, fearful, and crying, she clung to her mother's leg and whispered in a choked voice, "Mommy, I killed Uncle Mihai; he died because of my curses!"

Her mother looked down in astonishment, saw Lacrima, her eyes wide with the horror before them. She caressed her daughter's sweaty, feverish forehead, murmured a few strained words of comfort, and, without hesitation, lifted Lacrima in a consoling embrace, pressed her to her chest, and hurried home with her.

That day and in the following days, Lacrima did not attend kindergarten, and her mother didn't leave her bedside. First, she comforted Lacrima with a glass of milk and served her cinnamon semolina cookies. Then, she stroked her head, muttering sweet nothings. Throughout the night, she whispered words of comfort and tried to bring some order and reason to her daughter's nightmarish thoughts. Lacrima restlessly tossed in her bed, muttering incoherent phrases and crying out from her troubled dreams.

After several feverish days confined to her bed, with her parents taking turns to watch over her, Lacrima recovered and finally rose from her bed of nightmares.

While dressing, she smiled at her mother, who inadvertently hinted at a delightful surprise with her beautiful blue eyes.

Lacrima, skeptical of positive signs, scrutinized her mother's eyes again and detected a mysteriously joyful glint that seemed to foretell good news, enveloping her in a glow of boundless love and care.

"Guess who has a big surprise waiting in the large bedroom? Guess who has come back home healthy and whole?"

At her mother's words — words she had longed to hear — Lacrima didn't bother to finish buttoning her shirt and ran barefoot to her parents' bedroom to see her dearly missed beloved.

Through the bedroom door, she saw Lola, her Lolita, sitting in the middle of the bed in a new chiffon dress, purple and adorned with white velvet flowers. Overjoyed, Lacrima approached the bed and stretched out her arms to embrace Lola and kiss her beautiful china cheeks, but suddenly, her expression darkened.

This was Lola and yet it was not. She resembled Lola, with her wheat-blonde hair interwoven with strands of reddish burnished brass. Her eyes were blue but altered—cold, unfamiliar glassy blue eyes devoid of the warm, loving glow of the sky and the sea.

"This isn't Lola. Lola is dead. This is just a stupid china doll," Lacrima exclaimed, letting the cold, lifeless doll slip from her grasp. Moments later, she looked up, her eyes brimming with tears, and met her mother's gaze. Her expression conveyed profound disappointment and a total loss of trust. How could her mother deceive her like this?

As she stared at her mother in shock, tears streaming down her face, Lacrima caught her own reflection in the dresser mirror opposite her parents' bed. Reflected alongside her were the "Tears of Our Lady" flowers, drinking thirstily from the vase on the dresser. They shed their endless tears alongside hers, mourning humanity's sins and the eternal sufferings of her son, who was sacrificed to atone for them.

Lacrima returned her gaze to the mirror, where a little girl with black curls falling onto her sweaty brow stared back —a pale, unrecognizable stranger. Her normally greenish eyes were wide open, their color now a deep green, highlighting the darkened depths that harbored a sinister secret, forever dimming their light.

Was it real life or just fantasy

Pnina Tel Dan

A Good Place

Inspired by "A Small, Good Thing" by
Raymond Carver

January, in the dreary early afternoon of Jerusalem. The chill bit into the exposed body parts, sneaking through many layers of clothing and seeping into the bones, freezing their marrow. Hearts beat heavily. Blood congealed in partly blocked arteries. The city views were blurred, as if seen through inflamed eyes. The light was yellowish, dusty, and hazy. The air in Jerusalem was as murky as soured wine, making both breathing and the breath of life difficult.

The MAR Institute — offering imaging services for patients with respiratory and cardiac conditions, and for those suffering from fractures — sat atop the steep incline of Harav Kook Street.

Harav Kook Street adjoined the Jaffa Pedestrian Mall. On normal days, the pedestrian mall thrived with the bustle of café patrons and the joyful voices of diners in the scattered restaurants, the conversations of lovers, and the noise of families strolling with their children. To an observer, everyone seemed healthy, happy, and full of life.

Now, even the pedestrian mall lay deserted under a low, gray sky.

Approaching Harav Kook Street from Jaffa Street, one would encounter a narrow, deserted alley lacking in both accessibility and parking. It remains unclear why a medical imaging institute, of all places, should be here, forcing those who are disabled or otherwise impaired to battle accessibility issues to reach the impressive building clad in Jerusalem stone. The building, exuding dignity and innovation and housing cutting-edge technology, posed a challenge for those needing to enter its gates. The patients, except for the fortunate few with severe disabilities who had disabled parking permits, struggled bitterly with the trials of public transportation and the twisting, sloping alley leading up to the MAR Institute.

The walk up the street was resistant, defiant, unyielding. And as if that wasn't enough, the often malfunctioning building elevator forced those who visited to contend with a winding staircase that led down to the reception rooms and further down to the examination and imaging niches, safely located in the dark cellars of the technological institute.

A short-statured woman in her mid-fifties, dressed in a green coat, chubby and amiable-looking, arrived exhausted and full of worry at the crowded reception desk, filled mostly with elderly patients. They all stood like worshippers in prayer — or rather, like casino patrons before a slot machine, waiting for their lots to come up for an appointment with the receptionist, and from there to the examination rooms.

Due to the commotion, the worried woman, who seemed detached from both time and place, failed to hear the young woman calling her name, and missed her number displayed on the electronic screen opposite her. Realizing she had missed her turn, she shook herself and approached the receptionist. The indifferent deity behind the counter looked at her with expressionless eyes and explained that although the woman had a financial commitment from the HMO, meaning she had paid for a specialist consultation, she lacked a doctor's referral. Without one, they would have to reschedule her appointment.

Perplexed, she wanted to call her husband, who had parked far from the building, but then remembered she had left her phone at home. About fifteen minutes later, her savior arrived — a vigorous man, well-preserved with cheerfully brown eyes, in his early sixties. The man, sporting a short military-style haircut, soothed his agitated wife. After learning about the delay, he rummaged through his bag, found the cardiologist's referral, and energetically dealt with the bureaucratic paperwork that would allow his wife to proceed with the examination.

A voice emerged from the depths of the earth: "Hedva Sasson to the examination room, please." The plump woman in green recoiled, surprised, then collected her purse and coat. Struggling, she lifted herself from the chair to locate the source of the voice. After wandering back and forth, she saw a coiling staircase spiraling downwards toward the voice, which kept calling her name in a monotonous tone. For a moment, she was certain she was participating in a game of hide and seek, and the voice was slowly guiding her to the hiding spot where her playmate was concealed.

Finally, she and her husband arrived at a windowless corridor that served as an entrance to a double door decorated with skull-and-crossbones symbols, signifying an imminent threat of death or radioactive danger. Below, a statement in English identified the space as the "Laboratory for stress myocardial perfusion and isotope imaging." A healthy-looking man in his thirties, wearing white scrubs, waited for them at the open door — a Bennett-like friendlier version of a treatment room orderly.

"Hello, Hedva, I'm Moshe, and I'll be preparing you for the cardiologist's examination." His puffy lips stretched into a smug smile, masquerading as hearty friendliness. His Cheshire cat grin seemed to channel the whimsical world of Alice, striving desperately to infuse Hedva with a good and relaxed mood.

Moshe led Hedva to an electronic scale, maintaining his infectious grin. "Let's see how much you've slimmed down today. Really, fifty-eight? I wouldn't have guessed you a day over forty," he remarked, his smile unwavering. "Are you a teacher?" he asked. When she inquired how he knew, he replied, "It's evident from your sense of humor," before forcefully inserting a formidable needle into the back of her left hand. The needle bent under his attempt to be both professional and efficient, and the angel in white responded to her surprised cry of pain with a smiling indifference.

When Hedva asked why he had so forcefully jabbed the needle into the back of her hand instead of her upper arm, a less sensitive area, Moshe explained that the cardiac mapping test required walking briskly on a treadmill. "The cardiologist needs to inject the isotope into your venous catheter while you're increasing your walking pace. The hand holding the treadmill is more stable. Body movement might cause the hazardous material to spill onto you, the doctor, and heaven forbid, even stain the floor," he added, winking at his own stale joke and glancing at the not-so-pristine floor of the room.

Hedva struggled to follow the logic of his explanations. Complaining seemed pointless — the needle and the pain were now a fact.

About fifteen minutes later, the cardiologist entered the room. A man in his mid-forties, with a French goatee, narrow, laughing black eyes, and a generously kind smile. "I'm Dr. Ephraim, and I'll be conducting your stress test," he introduced himself cheerfully. He too did not skip the usual questions about Hedva's family status, medical history, and age, all the while completely ignoring the form in his hand that already contained all these details in black on yellow.

Dr. Ephraim placed the sensors on Hedva's body and cheerfully declared, "Hedva, the race begins now."

As Hedva gasped for air in desperation, feeling her lungs struggle futilely to inhale, sharp pains under her chest on the left side signaled that she had reached her limit of endurance. Just as she felt she was about to collapse; Ephraim administered the isotope injection. Hedva felt as if a thousand hydras — those mythical nine-headed, venomous serpents slain by Hercules — were unleashing their venom into her bloodstream. A burning heat swiftly gave way to a freezing numbness, followed by an uncontrollable shudder that folded her like a rag doll — much like the one her granddaughter played with. She resembled nothing so much as a marionette skillfully manipulated by a master puppeteer.

Despite the challenge, Hedva tried desperately to maintain her footing on the rapidly accelerating treadmill. A minute later, which seemed like an eternity, just before she was about to scream, "I can't take this anymore, I'm letting go of the handles," the ever-smiling Asclepius shed his light French demeanor, metamorphosed into a serious Greek demeanor, and increased the treadmill's speed. He sternly instructed Hedva to breathe properly. "Please ensure you inhale and exhale rhythmically, keep your mouth closed, and most importantly, do not let go of the treadmill handles."

Just before Hedva was about to give up and be flung to the back of the torture chamber, the test abruptly ended. The harrowing ordeal left her breathless, while in her ears, as if through a conch, the angel in white praised her for her bravery, her ability to reach the required heart rate, and her dignified endurance of what had been demanded of her.

With extra care, Hedva was removed from the torture contraption, which was connected to her and to a sophisticated computer that the cardiologist operated with excessive expertise and enthusiasm. The entire system and the examination process reminded Hedva of an article she had read in the "Haaretz" arts and culture supplement about sophisticated torture instruments, advanced for their time, that were discovered during archaeological excavations near the Colosseum in Rome. According to the newspaper, these devices were presumably used by the Roman Inquisition in the sixteenth century.

After shedding the cluster of sensors, Hedva was escorted to the waiting room to join other patients. Some had already been on the narrow path[17] of the ordeal, while others were still waiting for their turn. Everyone — those before and after the test — groaned as they struggled not to drown in the copious amounts of water they were instructed to drink continuously, one hour before and again for two hours following the test, until the completion of the cardiac scan with the gamma machine.

---

[17] On the Narrow Path (Ba-Mishcol Ha-Tsar): A novel by Hebrew-language author Aaron Abraham Kabak about the life of Yeshu, Jesus of Nazareth.

Still shaken and overwhelmed from the ordeal, Hedva settled into a plastic chair beside her husband, who was waiting for her in the corridor of what felt like a dungeon. To her, the corridor now seemed a sanctuary, a refuge for her and all the other survivors of the skull-and-crossbones chamber. Her somewhat unsettled gaze landed on an elderly couple, both over seventy and of Mizrahi descent, who were attentively listening to the words of an endearing old woman in her late eighties.

The endearing old woman's birdlike face was etched with wrinkles, and her transparent, light blue eyes were wide open with an expression reminiscent of a five-year-old child freshly scolded. Her body was frail and alarmingly gaunt. Her very upright posture reminded Hedva of a dry bamboo shoot, likely to snap with any careless movement. Very short, fluffy white hair adorned her small head, which sadly swayed from side to side on her long, withered neck.

The old woman spoke to the couple in her soft, thin voice, marked by a heavy Yekke accent — that distinctive German-influenced pronunciation common among Jews of Central European origin in Israel. Her voice, choked with tears, lamented the burial of her husband, who had died of heart failure about a month earlier. "My husband, Eliyahu, blessed be his memory, was a renowned professor in the Education Department at Hebrew University."

Many educators were mentored by him. He trained PhD students and teachers, wrote dozens of articles and books. He was also a senior advisor at the Ministry of Education, involved in shaping educational policies, and what did all his efforts yield? A pauper's burial in a third-floor niche in the wall — one of those above-ground compartments used in Israel due to limited space and high costs of traditional ground burials — nearly next to the fence".

"Enough, Mary, enough, may you know no more sorrow. God, blessed be His name, will comfort you, and when the Messiah comes, we shall all witness the resurrection together," Jacko consoled her.

Jacko was a gaunt, suit-clad man with a beret lazily perched on his silvery hair. His frail condition was evident in the way he leaned heavily on his wife, Tziona, who sat next to him. His voice carried a warm Moroccan-Jewish accent, and his deep-set, brown eyes, sunken into his hollow-cheeked face, looked kindly at Mary as she continued to express her indignation over her husband's burial. "I pleaded with Eliyahu to buy us a shared burial plot on the ground back when it was still possible to find a decent spot at a reasonable price," Mary continued to pour out her heartache to Jacko.

Jacko, noticing Hedva's intrigued glance, directed his words to both her and Mary, "Today, finding a burial spot on the ground is a luxury. A single grave in Jerusalem's largest cemetery, 'Har HaMenuchot' — the Mount of those who are resting — costs eighty thousand shekels, and a double grave in a prime location with a view can go for as much as two hundred thousand shekels. Who can afford such a thing? We are just simple people, pensioners. When the prices were reasonable, Tziona wouldn't hear of it. She told me, 'Not on your life,' afraid to hasten the end. And now, even at these insane prices, the wealthy snatch up every decent plot."

"True," Mary nodded, "Eliyahu also refused to buy a burial plot, unwilling to 'make these greedy Chevra Kadisha jackals any richer.' Now, after living together for over fifty years, we are to be buried separately, waiting for the Messiah's coming like animals in a disgraceful den. Tomorrow, our daughters arrive from the United States for the thirtieth-day memorial. How will we prostrate ourselves at the grave? How will we light candles? How will we honor his memory?"

Hedva, amused, barely contained her bursts of laughter that threatened to shake her entire body. "Sorry, but why should we provide a free feast for worms and also pay a fortune to the Chevra Kadisha? It's better to donate our bodies to science, then cremate the remains and scatter the ashes at sea," she said cheerfully, struggling to suppress her laughter.

Jacko joined in her laughter, drawing Tziona and Mary into the mirth. "You know, Tziona, in the end, we'll probably be buried in the Judean Foothills, where there's still enough land for graves. Isn't it a shame that our children might soil themselves in the mud if they come to visit us in winter at all? Who would travel that far? And if I die first, how will you manage to walk through the mud in winter when you come to light a memorial candle for me? Did you think about that? Maybe it really is better to donate our bodies to science or to some medical faculty lab. There, they'd keep us almost intact," he concluded, his laughter turning into a cough.

"Heaven forbid, what will happen when the Messiah comes? How will we rise for the resurrection?" Tziona asked, visibly shaken, glancing worriedly at her husband and Hedva, who were exchanging bursts of laughter.

"Hedva, please, be more considerate," her husband whispered urgently, gently nudging her side. "People believe in different things and might be hurt by your humor. Please, restrain yourself." His pleading look implored Hedva to stifle her laughter in the bud.

Tziona turned back to Mary, expressing empathy as she affectionately patted her shoulder. Like her husband, who suffered from arteriosclerosis and a weakened heart, she too was familiar with suffering from various ailments. A stout woman, her excess weight did not suggest robust health. In addition to diabetes, she had recently undergone a complex pelvic fusion surgery due to severe osteoporosis. Despite her frail physical state, she staunchly refused to use a walking cane. She maintained her dignity – never missing her weekly appointment with George, the neighborhood hairdresser. Her hair was meticulously dyed in warm honey brown shades by L'Oréal Paris, and her hairstyle was fashioned according to the latest trends.

"Why think about buying burial plots now? There's no need to invite trouble. After we've lived to a ripe old age, the children will inherit the house and with that inheritance, buy two adjacent burial plots on the ground," Tziona asserted.

"You are mistaken, Tziona," Jacko countered wearily, "Look at me and Eliyahu. It's better to sort these things out ourselves. We can't always rely on the children."

Jacko dropped his hand despairingly and said to his wife, "You'll see, Tziona, we'll end up being buried in some field in the Judean Foothills, in a secular burial site."

"Right, Jacko, may God have mercy, even that would be better than a niche in the wall. Now I'll need to climb a ladder each time to place flowers and light candles for Eliyahu's soul. At my age and with my health issues, one careless move, one unnecessary fracture, and I might end up in a niche just like him."

Mary shuffled slowly and waved her hand in farewell. "Thank you, Jacko, thank you, Tziona. May you live long and see much joy from your children and grandchildren. I'm off to say goodbye to the doctor. I'm done with the test, thank God. Goodbye."

"Poor thing," Tziona clucked sympathetically, "such an important and respected family. She has two daughters, prominent professors in education and early childhood psychology at Columbia University in the United States. They couldn't make it to their father's funeral, and she had to bury him alone. They will be here for the thirty days' memorial this week. It's tragic for her to be so alone at the end of her life, almost as if she were childless, without her daughters. To not see her grandchildren, not even on weekends. My grandchildren, God bless them, I see almost every day, thank God."

"Hedva to the imaging room, please." Moses interrupted the conversation and guided Hedva to the gamma camera bed. "The imaging will take about forty-five minutes," the friendly technician informed her as he positioned the sensors on her body. "You need to lie on your back and remain still and silent, or we'll need to repeat the process. It's challenging, but if you close your eyes and think positive thoughts, the time will pass more quickly. Remember, do not move under any circumstances until I say you can."

The monotonous rotation of the gamma camera above Hedva's head evoked Edgar Allan Poe's "The Pit and the Pendulum" in her mind — *but Moses had advised thinking happy thoughts,* she thought... *the pendulum will make you move.* She commanded herself to think of a pleasant place. Closing her eyes, Hedva recalled the spacious, whitewashed house where she and her husband had vacationed in Greece when they were younger. The house, with its red-tiled roof and shutters painted a Mediterranean blue, resembled the other fishermen's houses on the beaches of Agia Kyriaki, near the endless white shore.

The picturesque, enchanting village where she had spent such wonderful times with Ronnie, her then-future husband, when they were young, healthy, and carefree.

The warm, pastoral setting where she now focused her mind, along with the fond memories, helped her relax. Time sped by, and the scan proceeded without any issues. "That's it, Hedva, we're done. I'll help you get off now," Moses announced as he assisted Hedva from the machine. "I didn't even notice that forty-five minutes had passed," Hedva exclaimed, surprised. "Well, time flies when you're having fun," Moses quipped, returning to his earlier light-hearted tone and stale jokes.

After the draining test, before leaving the institute, Hedva peeked through the door and noted the intensifying frigid chill outside. The sky, cloaked in coal-black clouds, threatened to pummel the scurrying humans below with clumps of black hail, seeking refuge from the impending storm. The relentless rain seemed determined to drown them anew in a second biblical deluge, refusing to relent and reveal the forgiving spectrum of the rainbow.

The indifferent patriarch concealed his face in the heavens. Deep in the basement, in a world below where no place was lower, except where flowers could only be smelled from their roots, it remained cozy and warm.

Hedva nearly longed for the windowless lobby, where, amidst the red plastic chairs and facing the silently flickering television, she had experienced bursts of laughter that nearly overwhelmed her, spreading a morbid yet cheerful camaraderie not only to Jacko but also to other patients. They all sought reasons to unload the burdens of life and the anxieties of their test results.

"Behold how good and how pleasing for patients to sit together in unity," she mused, adapting the familiar Hebrew song to their situation. In the comforting warmth of the basement, a sense of shared fate enveloped them, inspired by Messianic visions — a longing for a better place in the Har HaMenuchot.

A place overlooking earthly Jerusalem from above — that terrestrial Jerusalem which echoes its celestial twin, the heavenly Jerusalem — with its breathtaking views. A place near the family. A place where the paths are paved and where the children might visit even on a rainy winter day like this — a day on which "Our Father who art in heaven" remained aloof, cold, accusatory, and distant, hidden behind his dark clouds.

Acknowledgments

I have been blessed with literary magnolias from the Thursday Reading Club, who diligently read my manuscript. Their wise and fruitful comments assisted me in bringing it to its current form. For this, I shall be eternally grateful to them.

My heartfelt thanks go to my talented daughter, Shira Tel Dan Feinerman, who read some of the short stories in their early versions and contributed to their improvement with her insightful remarks.

A special thank you is dedicated to Reuben Tel Dan, the man by my side, whose support, Sisyphean reading of the manuscript in its various versions, and judicious comments are invaluable.

My deepest thanks to my editor Stanley D. Hartzvi, whose sensitive, professional, and dedicated editing created magic and brought my book to fruition.